From the Splendid Sun to the Glorious Pound

Yusuf Sultan

To Dr Ann Thompson
Enjoy the adventure!
From, Yusuf Sultan
24th October 2023.

Acknowledgements

Thank you to Arif Majothi for the cover design, Dr Ann Thompson for editing the manuscript and Arif Javid for proofreading. Without their constant support and advice, this book would not have been possible.

To my family, who showed patience and forbearance when I was not able to give them as much time as I would have liked because of the demands of the book, my heartfelt thanks and love.

Copyright © Yusuf Sultan 2023

All rights reserved. No part of this publication may be reproduced, stored in a retrieval system, or transmitted in any form or by any means, electronic, mechanical, photocopying, recording or otherwise without the prior permission of the author.

Contact: yusufsultanmedia@gmail.com

In loving memory of my father
Saleji Ahmed Patel

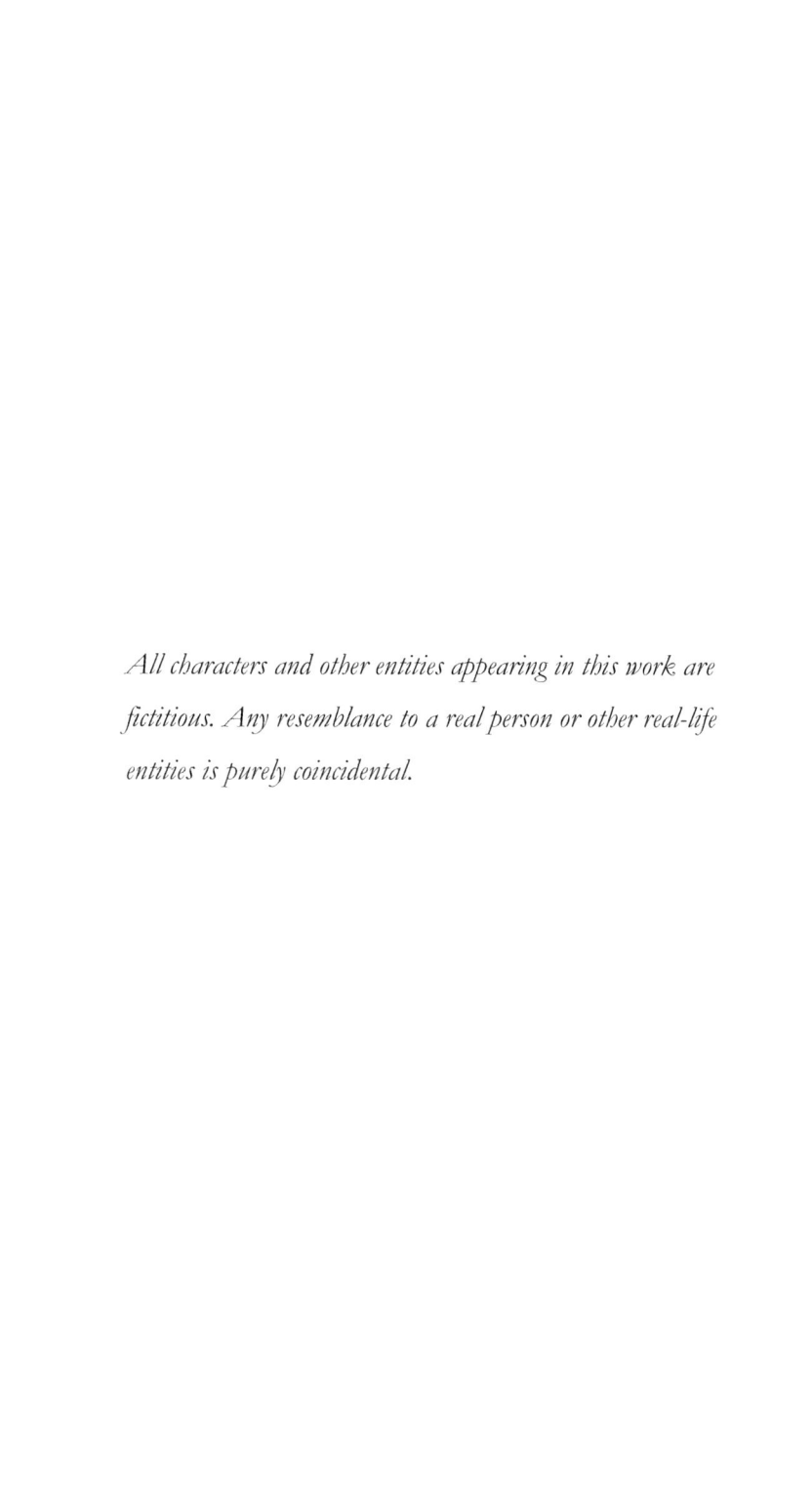

All characters and other entities appearing in this work are fictitious. Any resemblance to a real person or other real-life entities is purely coincidental.

Overview

As British Colonial rule in India declined, it left the country in a poor economic state and, following Independence, India's economic growth was painfully slow and had to face many challenges. India was divided into various states at the time of Independence and the most important challenge was to unify and integrate the country into one, to set up a democracy and a parliamentary-based government at the same time as eradicating corruption, poverty, unemployment and communal conflicts between Hindu and Muslim which have occurred since the period of British colonial rule and sometime leading to serious inter communal violence. The priority for the Indian government was to ensure the development and well-being of the entire population.

Economic ties continued between India and Britain. When India became a member of the Commonwealth and Britain needed a cheap labour force in its growing textile industries, migrants from the Commonwealth countries were invited to come to work in Britain. In return, the migrants worked unsociable hours, had to face many problems of overcrowding, and come to terms with dark, cold winter weather. Leaving their colourful country with the glorious sun behind, they faced racial discrimination and financial hardship because they had to send money back home to their families and to save money to invite their families to join them and stay here permanently.

As the years passed by, their quality of life in Britain with their families started improving and they became part of a close-knit community like the villages back home. Their dreams and ambition of a better future in Britain had paid off and now they had to face another challenge: a new generation of British Asians growing up in the UK. They had to face the issues of the generation gap. However, their sheer determination to move on equipped them to face the most difficult challenges ahead.

CHAPTER ONE

The Village, Poverty, Calm and Peaceful

In the village, the majority of Gujaratis lived in a close-knit community, where the elders played particularly important roles in the decision-making process. Most of the villagers were farmers, growing rice, lentils, wheat, barley and vegetables for domestic use and trading. The inhabitants of the village mostly lived in houses made of clay and bamboo and a few who were better off lived-in houses made of bricks.

The main form of transport consisted of ox or horse-drawn carts and there was one car: an Austin that was made in Britain, belonging to a family composed of rich landlords. A life of affluence and of luxury was a tall order for most people, whose furniture was simple: wooden chairs and beds made from jute strings. Although life was harsh for the poor, due to their traditional culture of staying close to extended family and having a close-knit community, they rarely faced social isolation. Attending Mosque contributed to the spiritual life, especially for the elders, and regular visits to friends and families alongside the open space of being in the village restored tranquillity to their lives.

Sufism, also known as "tasawwuf" in the Arabic-speaking world (from Islamic mysticism that emphasises introspection and spiritual closeness with God) was a common practice amongst many. People would gather in groups, a few would be seated in a circle on the ground whilst a delegated individual would provide the slow rhythmic beating of an Arabic drum. Religious poems would be chanted, and a volunteer would synchronise his body to the tune of the drum. As the chanting and the beat of the drums grew louder, the further he would descend into his trance, his body as the puppet and the beat as the puppeteer. Suddenly a long needle driven by his hand would make its way from one cheek through to the other, similarly, he would stab his stomach with a metal spike - no blood in sight - and rub it with hot ashes from the live fire to prevent infection. Although this kind of practice only took place once or twice a year, it was later prohibited by Islamic Scholars as being haram (forbidden).

The Muslims who lived here and in surrounding areas

The Village, Poverty, Calm and Peaceful

had a different appearance They had darker skin or light skin, and some were very white with blue or grey eyes. There are no historical records of how and when these Muslim inhabitants settled here, nor did they question their past. For generations their predecessors passed on verbal information which gave them some idea that most of them had reverted to Islam from Hinduism which they embraced happily

Traditionally the ancient history of Gujarat was enriched by the commercial activities of its inhabitants. So, there is historical evidence of trade and commercial ties with Egypt, Bahrain, and the Persian Gulf between 1000 and 750 BCE and traders used to come to Surat the main port which is 69.5 km from the village. The Muslims and the Portuguese came as traders in the 12th and 15th centuries, and the British also landed in Surat in 1608, as the surrounding area was intensively cultivated with chief crops including cotton, millet, pulses, and rice. In 1573, Akbar (1573-1605) the Emperor of the Mughal Empire captured Gujarat, and this explains how these Muslims were converted from Hindus to Islam, by the Muslims who came from overseas. It is also possible that over several hundred years, the overseas Muslims might have settled in Gujarat's districts, and hence they may have integrated with the locals, through marriages, socialisation, and trade.

Despite the harsh life, they all remained jovial. Their diet consisted of simple home-grown foods such as lentils and vegetables, meat was a rare luxury limited to once a week, whilst fresh fish was cheaper and easier to obtain from the river that would flow through the village. As they were just about managing to survive, having a materialistic lifestyle was out of the question. Family life was simple, they would sit on the floor and eat together with the food being cooked on an improvised home-made clay chulha (stove). The chulha was used for cooking almost everything and is still a tradition in many regions of rural India.

Although a clay chulha required you to flame it by blowing air continuously through a pipe and the clay cookers were lit with wood from the bushes, the food cooked on it was much tastier and healthier. Meat was very expensive, but they would occasionally buy goat which was the preferred meat. Sheep meat was frowned upon as, traditionally, it was regarded as unhealthy for humans, due to the Indian belief that the human body consists of cold and warm health conditions. As sheep meat was deemed "cold," it was

The Village, Poverty, Calm and Peaceful

regarded as bad for the joints. Beef was regarded as a delicacy, but it was illegal to consume it because the cow is an animal sacred to Hindus, who believe it is their Guy Mata (Mother Cow). Although Muslims did respect this, there was always the temptation to eat and so a few braver ones would discreetly kill a cow in the middle of the night and people would buy and cook it before dawn.

Overall, family life was harmonious but the future for the children was not promising as the economy was growing painfully slowly and, hence, poverty throughout India was going to last a long time and the chances of having a better future were very bleak. Like many anti-colonial struggles fought under the banners of self-determination, India led a similar struggle against the British Raj, but by using peaceful means, as adopted by Mahatma Gandhi, Mohammed Ali Jinnah who became the Prime minister of Pakistan after the partition and Jawaharlal Nehru who was the Prime minister in the 1960s. After Independence, the greatest challenge to both India and Pakistan was how to feed their growing populations, so like others who emigrated to the UK with great difficulties, there was insufficient finance for them to pay for the journey.

From the Splendid Sun to the Glorious Pound

In the village there was one school that provided education in Gujarati and Hindi where the children would sit on a floor plastered with clay. Islamic education was covered at the same school which turned it into a makeshift Madrasa (Islamic religious school) in the afternoon where they were taught religion and the Urdu language. After the age of twelve, pupils at the Madrasa would leave but continued attending School till age fifteen. After that the brighter boys attended further education only available in other towns and cities. The girls were expected to stay at home and learn the domestic duties in a large household and learn the skills of being housewives and sustaining marriages. The marriages were arranged by the elders at the early age of fifteen and in many cases, the family would already have made up their minds to marry them to cousins in the extended family or other relatives. These traditions were inherited over many years with the object of keeping whatever wealth they had within the family, alongside the provision of moral support. In some cases, villagers might marry someone from another village if the family had a social relationship with them.

Life remained simple and non-materialistic, and people would normally control their own family and community life.

The Village, Poverty, Calm and Peaceful

They had the benefit of good weather with the sun shining every day, the women folks would go out, work on farms, and wash clothes at the pollution-free river. Those who were slightly better off would supervise the peasants who were employed to work on farms and the workers were given food, some money and paid for their small weddings. The peasant men folks would work as labourers on farms. Their wives would carry out domestic tasks of bringing water from the water well, cleaning the houses and their children would take herds such as buffalo and cows to the river for washing and drinking water. The peasants lived as a small community nearby in small round mud huts and would sleep on the floor.

Amongst the farmers and some small traders there were people who were so poor that they were more concerned about where the next meal would come from and were resigned to the fact that they were born into poverty and will die as poor, so they blamed it on their bad luck and for many having the opportunity to emigrate to the UK was God sent. Everyone in the village knew everyone and in the event of instability within the family, the elders such as parents and grandparents would mitigate the effects, and if there were problems within the community, the village elders would find some solution. However, if there were any issues relating to the village, such as public facilities, the Sarpanch (village headman) appointed by the village body of local self-government called Gham Panchayat would deal with minor constructions, village roads or conflict within the community. The sarpanch is responsible for the overall development of the village and plays an important role in providing basic services such as the health and well-being of the villagers, drinking water and sanitation, the roles, and responsibilities of a Sarpanch were legally liable to organise Gham Sabha (village assembly) meetings. Every sarpanch is bound to organise a minimum of two Gham Sabha meetings on prescribed dates by the Government every year. The Sarpanch conducts all the Gham Sabha meetings. If there were any legal and criminal matters the Sarpanch would refer instruct the Patel to inform the Police or the appropriate local government authority in the nearby town or city. (Patel is an Indian surname, predominantly found in the state of Gujarat representing the community of land-owning farmers and businessmen) so once a person is elected as a Patel his family would inherit the name Patel for many generations to

The Village, Poverty, Calm and Peaceful

come. Patel can be Muslim or Hindu in Gujarat.

Here there is no threat of pollution from industries or road traffic, plenty of fresh air to breathe, organically grown food, meat from animals freely moved in the grass in open fields and Fish were caught from pollution-free rivers. As far as health was concerned the more prosperous ones would get treated by doctors. India did not have a welfare state like Britain and so in the event of any illnesses, the poor were treated by traditional herbalists and those who could not afford anything had to rely on home remedies. The main life-threatening diseases that hit them were TB (tuberculosis) for which there was no cure, and many used to die as a result, Smallpox Malaria and Typhoid used to be widespread and killed many people.

Whilst the poorer were more concerned about where the next meal would come from, in stark contrast the prosperous ones were enjoying a better quality of life with servants, better houses and businesses such as landowners. Few even owned travel agents' businesses established by parents in Bombay city and around towns and cities in Gujarat. They also got married at an earlier age where the parents chose the wife and a few years later after having children some got divorced and re-married because either they found a better match or simply did not get along. It also had a lot to do with being prosperous and some did pay for the welfare of the ex-wives and children. Some divorced wives were left at the mercy of their parents who brought up the grandchildren and few would have two wives living separately and be financially maintained in separate accommodations. The women lived as single parents and only a handful would remarry, and the children became the victims emotionally, but the father did provide money for their education and well-being.

In the western part of India, the Gujarat State consists of rural communities which have a long tradition of people emigrating to the African continent to seek a better future for their families. The British rulers recruited Indians to work on the expanding railway transport system in Africa and the Indians did well in many African countries because the Gujarati community started getting involved in trades such as opening shops and other initiatives that were warmly welcomed by the British government. After settling down, the British Asians invited their families to live there permanently. They set a good example for people in Gujarat

The Village, Poverty, Calm and Peaceful

who were quick to realise the benefits of immigration, so they too were inspired to go abroad, but this time in a different direction. They chose Britain.

In 1962, fifteen years after India became independent from the British Raj in 1947, India was facing huge problems with a rising population and poverty, and it was difficult for the Indian government to provide all the necessary support for people to have a better quality of life. Therefore, the best thing they could do was to go abroad. Britain seemed the obvious choice, simply because after the Second World War there was a labour shortage there. The British government invited foreign nationals from the Indian subcontinent to work in the textile factories, in engineering and in transport, with promises of British citizenship, a free health service and free education for their children. In India, the local travel agents and the government officials had never had it so good because it created opportunities for them to make a vast amount of money through bribery. People had to go through the bureaucratic process to obtain visas for Britain and, as they were victims of poverty and had no prospects of a better future for their children in India, they had no alternative other than to pay a vast amount of money to

From the Splendid Sun to the Glorious Pound

escape to the promised land, Britain. Furthermore, the villagers had already witnessed how soon the people who had already settled in Britain managed to pay off the debt which they had accrued in going to Britain and how they had already arranged for their families to join them. Even the middle classes encouraged their sons to go to the UK after completing their further education, due to the lack of social mobility and poor prospects of a better future in India.

Those who used to work on farms in the villages got jobs in textile factories in the UK and were living happily. At the weekend they would wear suits (their experience in the textile factories led to quality fabrics such as mohair, wool, and gabardine as the suit fabrics of choice), shirts, shoes, and a tie which they had never dreamed of in the village. They almost looked like English gentlemen: clean-shaven with Brylcreemed hairstyles, looking affluent, they would go to have their photograph taken in a studio. This was to be sent to their families who would have it framed and displayed in the house back in India. Extended family members and friends seeing this photograph would be pleasantly surprised to learn how life had been transformed for them, from struggling farmers to prosperous-looking gentlemen - at least according to Indian standards. This further inspired them too to go to Britain without hesitation, requesting their friends or family members to send them a work permit. There were promises of a better quality of life awaiting them in the UK and they did not stop to consider the cold weather or the other difficulties they would face there.

From the Splendid Sun to the Glorious Pound

CHAPTER TWO

This Is Not Just About Me

Amongst the hopefuls was Bashir aged 30 who lived in a small village in Gujarat with his wife Amina and two children, Ahmed aged 11 and Jameela aged 6. They, like many others, contemplated going to Britain to seek an improved standard of living and escape the poverty all around them. Bashir had to borrow money from the rich landlords for a visa, in return for which he had to loan his farming lands until he had earned enough money in Britain to pay it back. He would regularly make the trip to see a travel agent ten miles from his village, but he had made several trips in the last six months with no success in obtaining a visa for Britain. It had already cost him huge amounts for the advance payments and bribes. This created financial hardship and all he had were promises from the agent reassuring him that it would not be long before he got his visa. Like the others, he had no alternative other than to wait.

One day Bashir was working on the farm under the blazing hot sun with an ox- pulled implement, digging soil in the afternoon. It was nice and quiet, with only the sound of the birds in the background. Suddenly he heard his son Ahmed's excited voice coming towards him. Ahmed handed him an envelope which the postman had just delivered, and Bashir opened it without any hesitation. He could not believe his eyes, he looked at his son in amazement. The visa had arrived, and the travel agent had confirmed that he was to leave on a B.O.A.C. (British Overseas Airways Corporation) flight in two weeks. He rushed to see his wife and broke the good news to her. She was happy that their venture for a prosperous future was heading in the right direction, but had mixed feelings, because they would not be able to see each other for a few years. Bashir and Amina decided not to tell anyone about the flight apart from close family members, out of fear of others, who might try to prevent him from travelling due to jealousy or try to jump the queue by bribing the travel agent with higher amounts of money. Now, the main task was to organise the packing of the luggage for the journey and to leave some money for the family, enough to survive on for at least a few months until Bashir was settled in Britain and had started earning some money.

Two weeks later he said farewell to his wife, the children,

This Is Not Just About Me

and parents and, although it was a happy occasion, knowing that they would not be able to meet for a couple of years made it difficult, particularly when the family did not have a tradition of going away to such a far location. He decided to leave in the middle of the night just before dawn so that nobody would find out. His wife had packed some food for the journey, he also took a lit paraffin lamp as he had to walk through farms in the dark for about two miles to catch the train to Bombay. Bashir took a last glance at his wife who came into the yard quietly to say farewell and he started walking. For Bashir, there was no looking back he was now ready to face the biggest challenge of his life, and the only precious thing he was carrying with him were memories of his beloved family. He finally got to the railway station as the morning was brightening up and as he no longer needed the lamp, he gave it to a beggar who was sleeping on the ground.

The local train had arrived, and Bashir sat near the window having a last look in the direction of his village. The train was steaming through Gujarat and an hour later they arrived at the mainline railway station in Bilimora, where he was to board another long-distance train to Bombay. Bashir had an hour to wait before boarding the train, so he sat on the platform and saw a chaiwala (a man selling some tea) so he bought some tea and ate samosas (spicy pasties filled with Chicken and vegetable) and bhajias (Indian spicy cutlets made with chickpea flour) which his wife had cooked for breakfast. He was enjoying watching the other passengers: some young men were singing; people were selling food and there was a chaiwala (hot tea seller) paniwala (a person selling water) all yelling at the tops of their voices. It was a typically amusing scene at an Indian railway station and time passed quickly. Finally, the train was seen approaching the station and there was a mad rush for people to secure their seats. Thankfully, Bashir had a coolie (a man who would carry the luggage for passengers and jump on to the train to save seats, quite normal in India) who managed to secure a seat for Bashir in the second-class compartment. Bashir paid him his fees and then he sat in the overcrowded compartment. The steam train slowly started moving and Bashir watched the other passengers who were enjoying themselves singing and reading as well as asking each other about their castes which is generally known in India to determine the status of a person. They were having fun, and Bashir also joined the conversations but did not volunteer any information about

This Is Not Just About Me

going to the UK, in case someone knew people in his village.

As the train approached Bombay Central station, people rushed to get off. Bashir was going to be met by his friend Suleman who was waiting outside at the gate. Suleman had advised Bashir in advance to hold tight to his luggage because of the numerous conmen who would pretend to assist with carrying the luggage only to rob the passengers of their items. After greeting each other Suleman took Bashir to a tanga (a horse-drawn taxi) because it was cheaper than a car. Bashir had a cultural shock looking at the traffic, hearing the continual car horn sounds, seeing the busy streets with their tall buildings and packed full of so many people. Finally, they arrived at Suleman's flat and, after freshening up, they rested for a while. Suleman then took Bashir to a restaurant, which was like a cafe, and they had some food. Bashir found this place very interesting with its different types of people from different religious backgrounds and using different Bombay dialects. In the evening, Suleman took him to the famous seaside area known as Chowpatty beach where people from all over India would visit when they toured Bombay. Here, the street food was a real delicacy, and they did not waste time enjoying it all to the background sound of the sea.

Later, they travelled back to the flat in a tram and on the way, Bashir enjoyed passing by the busy nightlife of Bombay. Suleman told Bashir that the next day he would take him to the famous Chor Bazaar which is the largest flea market in India and one of the tourist attractions of Bombay. The word Chor means thief and, according to popular legend, if you lose anything in Bombay you will be able to buy it back from the "Chor Bazaar." So, the next day Bashir bought some second-hand winter clothes from the Chor Bazaar to wear in the UK. Later on, Suleman took him on a tour of Bombay city and Bashir bought some presents. "Bombay Halwa" (a sweet similar to Turkish delight with almonds and pistachios) is a delicacy that people's friends and families would expect from someone visiting Bombay. So, he bought some for family and friends which Suleman had agreed to send with a fellow worker who was going to a village near Bashir's the next day. He also bought some for his cousin and friends in the UK. In the evening, Suleman and Bashir went to the cinema and afterwards went to a restaurant, where they enjoyed a nice meal. They had an early night as Bashir was to fly in the morning. Bashir tried to sleep but

This Is Not Just About Me

found it difficult as he was already missing his family.

Meanwhile back in the village, his wife Amina was trying to get into the daily routine of caring for the children and her father and mother-in-law without Bashir. Being without her husband left her constantly anxious as they had been married for twelve years without being away from each other. Many thoughts went through her mind: what if something goes wrong with his visa and he cannot travel? How will he cope once he is in the UK because he has always worked on a farm and has never had to iron clothes or cook? Are the cracks appearing on the ceiling and walls going to lead to a collapse of the building if nothing is done to repair it in a couple of years? Then she looked at the children and tried to put her negative thoughts behind her, looking ahead to a better future. She tried not to be sad in front of the children and instead would cry alone at night.

The next morning, Suleman and Bashir got up early and after having breakfast they got into a taxi and left for the airport. They had to wait for about two hours but then Bashir said farewell to Suleman and after going through Customs, he finally boarded the plane. He settled down in his seat and tried to fasten his seat belt but was struggling as this was the first time he had been on a plane. Thankfully, the air hostess came and helped him. He had already spoken to some passengers around him and found that women and kids were travelling to join their husbands, and some like him were going for the first time. Also, for the first time, he came across some white people. Bashir felt at ease and was convinced that going to Britain was the right choice.

Soon the plane started to take off and Bashir had his last look at Indian soil. It was a different world for Bashir, but the white air hostesses made passengers comfortable with welcoming gestures and later started serving food and showing an English movie which Bashir enjoyed afterwards, like many other passengers, Bashir had a nap and after a few hours, the plane started its descent into Heathrow Airport. After disembarking the plane Bashir could feel the cold in the wet, winter weather. He managed to get through Customs without any difficulty. The officers were welcoming and had interpreters who could speak Hindi and Urdu. He was travelling with only light luggage because his cousin had told him not to buy too many clothes, and he was only carrying thirty-five pounds in currency because that was the limit the Indian government had imposed for people going abroad. Bashir was a bit nervous because he had never ventured out of Gujarat let alone abroad.

He was met by his cousin Ismail who was waiting for him and when Bashir saw him, he felt a great sense of relief. His first impression of the airport was somewhat different from that of Bombay Airport, everyone was walking greeting each other quietly and no one shouted out with the excitement of seeing the passengers. Ismail did hug him and welcomed him with some excitement but quietly. Having been living in the UK for the last three years he had got used to not attracting too much attention and not disturbing others. Bashir was so surprised to see Ismail looking so different - dressed in a dark suit, tie, and long warm overcoat. He was looking well. Even his skin colour looked lighter due to the winter season, and he did not show any signs of being stressed.

Despite the many layers of warm clothing that Bashir had bought in Bombay, he was feeling very cold. Ismail had brought with him a warm winter overcoat and scarf, which was a great relief for Bashir. They got into a tube train heading to King Cross station, Bashir sat quietly because by this time he had realised that the culture of travelling was very disciplined, unlike in India. For the first time in his life,

From the Splendid Sun to the Glorious Pound

Bashir noticed a few passengers who were from different races and backgrounds. Ismail and Bashir got off at Kings Cross station and were about to board the train to Leeds when Bashir became rather puzzled upon seeing that apart from a handful of porters there were no coolies, no mad rush, no overcrowded trains. People were carrying their own luggage and the station was quieter than in India. As the train started moving, Bashir and Ismail sat in a compartment along with white passengers who were sitting reading or quietly minding their own business, whilst politely looking and smiling. Bashir being Indian and not being from a culture of travel in which quietness is emphasised, started talking with Ismail in a loud voice. To Bashir's surprise the white passengers did not mind, and he was pleasantly surprised.

As the train passed through the countryside, he started seeing barren agricultural lands and trees without any greenery. The sky was dull with snow. Ismail told him they were in the winter months and the whole of England became like that but in spring it would be nice and green. As the train approached Yorkshire, he noticed some dark chimneys on the houses as well as tall industrial chimneys

This Is Not Just About Me

next to large factories throwing out dense smoke. Bashir was curiously thinking and asked Ismail what the chimneys were for, so Ismail informed him that it was from the burning of coals to keep the houses warm, and that the large, tall chimneys belonged to textile factories. He told Bashir that after a good rest and an enjoyable weekend, by Sunday evening they would start thinking about the tall factory's chimneys, which, Ismail said, was not a pleasant reminder for Monday when they would have to go to work. But Ismail reassured Bashir that these factories were the future livelihood for them and their loved ones, so there was no looking back. Bashir remembered when he used to hear back in the village how those who had already settled in the UK improved the quality of life for their families back home and Ismail was the living proof of such an achievement.

The train arrived in Wakefield, West Yorkshire after about five hours. Bashir was once again surprised to see that there was no mad rush and the passengers got off in an orderly manner. Even outside on the platform there was no noise nor entertaining crowds, nor Indian coolies to carry luggage for passengers so Ismail helped him. As they got outside to queue for the taxi, Bashir had his first taste of the cold wind

From the Splendid Sun to the Glorious Pound

and falling snow. He stood nervously on the snow trying to figure out how hard it was and found it slippery so, to his relief, Ismail took him by the arm, and they headed towards the taxi rank. They got a taxi to Dewsbury which took about forty minutes. Bashir was rather puzzled to see such intense darkness so early in the afternoon.

They arrived at the house and parked on a cobbled street. Bashir noticed the house was stone-built, almost black (due to the age of the stone which turns darker with the weathering) and with the weather being dark, cold, and miserable, a complete contrast to Indian weather. Ismail knocked on the door and Hassan one of the tenants opened it. When they got into the house Bashir had a warm welcome from the other tenants who were from his village. After freshening up, Bashir sat with them enjoying a nice cup of tea. The house was back-to-back with only one room downstairs containing an old worn-out sofa, some chairs, a sink, a small cabinet, a gas cooker, and a small dining table. There was a massive black fireplace made of iron, burning coals and the floor was covered with a worn-out vinyl floor covering. Bashir realised that all three of them looked healthy and happy, whereas he was very thin.

This Is Not Just About Me

They made Bashir comfortable and sat down to talk and, after asking him about his journey, the tenants were interested in catching up on the news about their families and friends back home. They did not waste any time in asking Bashir about the Bombay halwa which was promptly handed over and immediately enjoyed with a warm cup of spicy tea. Later Bashir wanted to use the toilet so Yunus, one of the tenants, walked with him into the narrow alleyway and down a couple of steps, and showed him the toilet which was outside at the back of the house. He was given a jug with warm water for washing afterwards. The toilet cabin was made of wood and a draught was coming under the gap between the door and frame. The floor was covered in frost - extremely cold and slippery. He had to learn to put each foot on the edge of the toilet wall in a balancing act. He was nervous as, back at home, he was used to using an Indian toilet and took care not to slip and fall. Later, they all ate the Biryani which the tenants had cooked (a delicacy cooked with rice, meat, lentils, yoghurt, and hot spices traditionally prepared for special occasions, for guests, religious festivals, weddings and so on) and in the cold weather, it was a real blessing. His friends teased him, "welcome to Britain brother

From the Splendid Sun to the Glorious Pound

Bashir, there are no wives here to cook for us you know." Bashir took it in his stride and laughed. Later in the evening one of the friends said goodbye because he had to start his night shift at the factory. Bashir had to sleep in a damp bedroom with frost-covered windows, where a cold draught would find its way through the cracked window frames, the bed was extremely cold, and the only source of heat was from a small portable electric heater with two bars.

They got up in the morning and had Indian-style omelettes for breakfast with toast and tea and some fruit. Afterwards, the first thing he did was to write a message to his family for a telegram confirming that he had arrived safely which Hasan would send at the post office. He also wrote a letter to his wife Amina in great excitement telling her about the journey, meeting friends, his hopes and dreams and although he talked about the bad weather and living conditions, he reassured her that it was all worth it. Finally, the dream of a new life had begun for Bashir, and he was ready to face the challenge ahead. There was no looking back.

Back at home, two days later the postman delivered a telegram to Amina which was in English, so she took it to a teacher at the school, who read it out in Gujarati and told her that Bashir had arrived in the UK safely. Amina's confidence grew day-by-day and her Islamic faith led her to pray for the protection of her family and Bashir against any obstacles so that everything would run smoothly. She was now just as determined as Bashir was to make a new life for themselves in the UK.

From the Splendid Sun to the Glorious Pound

CHAPTER THREE

Follow The Chimneys

Bashir was made to feel at home by his friends. They did not charge him for rent or food until they found him a job and even offered him money to send back home to his family. Bashir had to get used to the new routine of sharing the domestic tasks and learning to cook. In the early morning, Bashir was woken up by the noise of rattling bottles from the milk delivery float pulling up outside and the milkman leaving milk bottles on the doorsteps. This was in complete contrast to back home where his wife would go to the stable early in the morning to milk the buffalo and cows. Here, he had the luxury of milk in bottles along with sliced bread, fresh orange juice and eggs all delivered by the milkman. He saw a gas cooker for the first time but soon got used to it, he had to learn to light a fire just like his wife used to light the cooking stove back home.

Whilst his friends were at work, he was alone apart from the tenant who was sleeping after working a night shift, which meant he had to remain a bit quieter. He had lunch made up of the leftovers from the previous day and in the evening, he prepared some chapatis (round, flat, unleavened bread of India that is usually made of wholewheat flour and cooked on a griddle) as he had been taught by Amina for everyone.

Since he was not able to cook the main meals, his friends would cook in the evening after returning from work. All this, coupled with the cold, not being able to go out due to the dark weather, frost-covered pavements and the almost non-existent activity in the neighbourhood made it difficult to cope. Life was so different compared to back home. Despite all this, he remained happy. There were many positives: the food was plentiful, there was lots of different fruit, far more meat consisting of chicken, lamb, and beef (and no religious restrictions in the UK). The only problem for them was that Indian tropical fruits and vegetables were unavailable, so despite having to make do with English vegetables they were still able to cook spicy Indian style food. After Bashir had arrived in the UK, he further realised just how his friends had given their families a good quality of life by sending money back home and inspired him to think ahead and settle here with a job.

On Friday morning there was a knock on the door, and it

was an Englishman with six live chickens in a sack with holes in it (so the chickens could breathe) which the residents would buy every week. One day whilst they sat having breakfast there was a very loud noise from outside and down in the cellar as if a wall had collapsed. Ismail told him not to worry, and that it was men who were shovelling coal down the chute into the basement, which they would use for the coal fire. Bashir went outside to see for himself and was once again surprised to see white men with faces blackened from the coal dust doing such manual labour – quite a contrast from the British colonials who would never be found doing such work in India. Previously, Bashir had seen the milkman delivering milk, bread and eggs and the day before he had seen the dustbin men collecting the rubbish and other white men repairing the road. All this seemed incredible to him because, back home, the British were 'superior' to them and known as Saab (sir or master) and would make Indians do the menial work. Bashir realised that white workers were just like the working-class native Indians who did hard manual labouring back home.

The next weekend when the residents were at home and cooking, Ismail took Bashir to town in the morning to show him around and do some shopping. As they were walking, Bashir found it extremely cold. The fog and grime from the chimneys made the day even darker. Ismail told him that the town would be busy because of the Christmas festival but it was nothing like the colourful festivals back home. The buildings were stone-built and very dark, people were dressed in layers of warm, dark clothes and the only similarity he found were the people selling fruit and vegetables in the market, displaying their goods, and yelling to attract customers. However, he enjoyed seeing the colourful Christmas lights displayed in the streets and the festive songs played in shops, along with the live music performed by the Salvation Army brass band in the open space. What Bashir found most interesting was that everything from food and items of clothing to household goods were available at prices which most people were able to afford. Like at Heathrow airport and the railway station, Bashir was again most impressed by people behaving in an orderly manner. He found that people would smile and queue up for shopping and there was no haggling over prices like back at home.

After shopping, they returned home and all sat down to

Follow The Chimneys

eat a lunch of spicy chickens and rice followed by warm rice pudding, which Bashir appreciated after shopping in cold weather. Their conversation mostly revolved around work, the better prospects in the UK and the letters they had received from families back home, a feel-good factor for them all. Afterwards, Bashir volunteered to wash the plates and pans. His first experience of doing domestic tasks had already begun with using the water taps, so it was not much of a problem. He also noticed the others washed their clothes in the improvised utility room in the cellar. Bashir had already begun to realise the tough challenges ahead of him, but there was also something entertaining waiting in the late afternoon. They all sat near the fireplace with a small black and white television in a corner and they would watch wrestling, which was the standard routine every Saturday. Bashir and his friends had never watched television back home in their village. They joked about how the English wrestlers were beating the hell out of each other and the friends would excitedly take the side of the "good" one and ridicule the followers of the "bad" one, whilst drinking Indian masala tea. They would get up and shout, a display of the typical behaviour that any highly adrenaline-fuelled spectator would indulge in. Sometimes, the picture quality would become a bit fuzzy so they would tap on the top of the TV which got it started again.

There was even more entertainment awaiting Bashir on Sunday morning. Yunus told him to get up at nine in the morning because they were all going to the cinema at eleven o' clock. They got up accordingly, had a clean shave and breakfast, and dressed in their best. It was almost customary to wear suits and ties and lapel pin badges, either B.O.A.C. (British Overseas Airways Corporation) or Air India, which they were given by the airlines when they got off the planes. This was a complete transformation from being farmers back home, and looking almost like English gentlemen, they went to the cinema. Bashir was puzzled when he heard the sound of loud church bells ringing from the church in town to signify it was time for the Christian worshippers to gather for the church services. This was a new experience for him because he had never come across Christians back home and when he asked the others about it, they told him that every Sunday the Christians would go to church to pray. Bashir suddenly realised something and asked if there were any mosques, they told him there were no mosques and only a handful of people would pray at home, because the migrants were all young and there were no elders who would normally remind them to pray at least on Fridays back at home.

Finally, they got to the cinema which had posters of Hollywood movies and next to them were some small posters of Indian movies. Asian businessmen would hire cinemas from ten o'clock in the morning to five o'clock in the evening, screening two movies, each three hours long. The audiences were both Indian and Pakistani and they almost used to get lost watching these movies. It was like being back home because the movies were about families, and communities, with wonderful locations and colourful romantic songs with the main hero and heroine romancing, mostly shot in remote villages, and this helped the audience to de-stress after working for a whole week. They would scream, and shout and some even sang along with the characters. Like the others, Bashir felt a sense of belonging to a community that was thriving according to Indian standards and so he started gaining more confidence and remained cheerful. After the movies, they would go home as there were no Indian restaurants to go to in the Dewsbury area. So, they cooked nice meals which they would normally eat on a festive occasion back at home.

Once a month they would go to Bradford, about twelve miles from Dewsbury and Batley, where they would see newly released Indian and Pakistani movies, because Bradford had a sizeable Pakistani community by now and there were a couple of restaurants where delicious traditional food was served. The restaurants would also cater for the textile workers who had no families here. They would eat their daily meals and pay every Thursday when they got their wages and, at weekends, the workers would also eat there after shopping or seeing movies. Bashir and his friends went to one restaurant and had some Kashmiri-style food, consisting of kebabs, meat or chicken curries, rice, naans or chapatis. It was all very tasty but hot and spicy, different to the Gujarati food. The jukebox blasting out Indian and Pakistani movie songs was a bonus.

Ismail had already booked two days' holiday so that he could help Bashir find a job. He reminded Bashir about the chimneys which they had talked about on their way from the airport and as they walked, Ismail pointed out the factories' chimneys and told him that they were to follow the chimneys to look for a job. They went to a few textile factories, but

Follow The Chimneys

they wanted experienced machine operators. Finally, there was one factory where the manager communicated through Ismail who could speak broken English and told Bashir that he had been offered a job as a trainee spinning machine operator with a reasonable weekly wage for two weeks then a full wage when he was fully trained. Bashir was overjoyed with such a happy surprise and felt that his dream of a new life with the family was coming true at last.

They came home and informed the tenants of the good news and they said that this called for a celebration and so Bashir volunteered to cook some rice and chicken curry which he had learnt from Ismail a couple of days before and took out some mango pickles which his wife had made from the home-grown mango trees back in Gujarat. They did not offer daily prayers, but Bashir remembered what his wife had told him about praying before going to find a job and after a job so that success would be granted by almighty God, so Bashir prayed to show gratitude for the new life he had been granted. Bashir immediately started writing a letter to his wife as he could not wait to tell her the most exciting news of the new chapter in their life and, with a sense of humour, he mentioned that he had learned to cook as well. On the whole, their faith in each other remained strong.

The next day, one of the tenants Abdul had an asthma attack so the doctor was called. The doctor, who was white, examined him with great care and prescribed some medication which Ismail went out to the nearby chemist to pick it up free of charge. Bashir was overly impressed by the friendly nature of the doctor and asked Abdul about the cost of the visit. Abdul told him that it was free of charge including the medicines because they all paid into the government's National Insurance contributions system. The government would deduct small amounts from their wages and, in return, no matter how expensive any treatment costs were (including hospitalisations or operations), it was all covered and subsidised by the government. Bashir now remembered what he had heard back home about the free health services in the UK. Later in the afternoon, Ismail took Bashir to see a friend who lived two miles away who had a minibus and took workers to the factory where Bashir had got a job and arranged for Bashir to be picked up on Monday.

The next day Bashir received a letter from his wife. The post would normally take two to three weeks to reach the

Follow The Chimneys

UK and it was always a pleasant moment when any of them received letters from back home and they could tease each other about their wives being romantic. She wrote a very emotional letter, about how much she, the children and the rest of the family were missing him and worrying about his well-being but added that she was at ease because Bashir had already written to tell her that he had friends who were taking care of him. She told him that they were all fine and still had some money left for food. Friends and family members had also offered to help if necessary. Bashir was content with the news from home and knew that when his wife received the second letter, she would be happy to learn about the job. At the weekend he enjoyed the same routine as previously and he also went to visit some of Ismail's friends and was introduced to them. It was normal practice to get to know fellow countrymen who would support each other morally and financially. The main reason for this was that there were very few people from India, probably about a couple of hundred settled in Dewsbury and Batley, about three miles from each other.

For Bashir and others, it was exciting to watch TV and listen to radio programmes from back home including pieces

From the Splendid Sun to the Glorious Pound

of music and the news, but they were only able to get it on a short- wave signal, so the quality was not really clear. They all took a keen interest in watching the news on TV which was often accompanied by a translation from one of the tenants. The news mostly covered the weather, domestic politics, the IRA, the Northern Ireland conflict and foreign news, news unheard of back home. Here they might also see news about a famine in India due to poverty, and how the British charity, Oxfam, was raising money to send to these poor people in India. Furthermore, they saw news about crimes in the UK and images of the bombing in the Vietnam war, which was alien to them. They were happy to learn that Britain was not taking part in the Vietnam war, and that they would not have to join the British Army. This coupled with the challenges of settling in the UK would have been a bit too much for them to cope with so, instead, they enjoyed watching positive stories about the Queen and the Royal family. Back home in Gujarat they did not have a tradition of joining the Army and very few joined the police forces. They were known to be part of a passive and peaceful community composed of farmers and tradesmen. Their main motto was to work hard, earn a living and mind their own business, and that was exactly what they set out to do in Britain.

On Monday morning Bashir got up, had breakfast, and made a packed lunch for work: some chapati wraps filled with chicken masala, some tea bags, milk, and an apple. It was a difficult task in the cold winter months. When he had done this, he heard the minibus pull up outside and he left for work. There were some eight other workers in the bus going to the same factory. The minibus was full of cold draughts coming in as the windows and doors had slight gaps-not very pleasant in frosty, bitter cold weather added to which the heater was not very warm. But Bashir did not worry about it too much as he saw the others sitting calmly and what could be better than going to earn money? On the way, they picked up two more passengers and soon they were all talking about the good time they had had at the weekend and soon got to the factory. The manager greeted him and introduced him to a supervisor who took him to a worker who would train him for about two weeks and teach him to operate the worsted yarn spinning machine. It was a complete contrast to working in open fields back home.

Here it was a huge department, with long machines, yarn baskets and everywhere was full of loud noise coming from the machines in the closed environment. Used to working in an open space farming back at home, he found the factory a bit claustrophobic at first but soon got involved in the training and started getting used to it. The trainer was a Pakistani immigrant Zahid who spoke Urdu, and Bashir had no problem because he had learnt Urdu and Hindi back home so he could communicate well. The workers at the factory were from different backgrounds. There were English men and women, Polish men and women, Indians, Pakistani men, and all were engaged in similar duties. Bashir found most of the white workers were friendly apart from one or two workers who thought that the immigrants had come to take their jobs. However, the majority were welcoming and once he started training, he felt much more comfortable. The only thing that worried him were the spindles revolving at high speed. The rotating wheels and the loud noise made him feel nervous and worried about hurting himself, but the trainer was aware of his trainee's fears at the beginning, and he reassured Bashir about the health and safety provisions in place.

In the afternoon there was a lunch break and Bashir collected the packed lunch he had brought from home. A fellow worker had advised him to put it on top of the powerful, warm lightbulb box at the end of the spinning machine (the bulb light would beam to identify any broken threads) to keep the food warm. He went to the canteen to eat where the white workers would eat bland English food, whilst the Asians would eat spicy Indian food which a few white workers did not approve of due to the strong smell. Furthermore, the Asians continued to feel that there were a handful of white workers who did not approve of the immigrants coming into the UK, mainly spurred on by the fear that they would be taking their jobs. In reality, this was not the case as the immigrants were invited to provide a cheap labour force because so many British soldiers and civilians had died in the Second World War and Britain was still going through the industrial revolution. As a result, the UK needed a labour force from abroad. However, this was the least of the Asian workers' worries because they were preoccupied with the thought of moving forward onwards and upwards and improving the quality of life for their families. Bashir had completed his training within two weeks and the supervisor approached him and told him the good news that he would be working as a spinning machine operator and handed him his weekly wages. He thanked the supervisor excitedly and, holding the wages in his hand he prayed to almighty God in thanks for this reward. Like the others he was now well on his way to settle in his chosen country. Later, as he was going home, he paid the minibus driver for the transport and when he got home, he offered to pay his fellow tenants for his board and lodgings, but they refused, advised him to send money to his family instead and told him to start paying them in two weeks.

As Bashir's confidence grew, he started going shopping alone in town as he wanted to get to know more places and people and would go to the movies alone on Sunday when the others could not make it. He was careful with his money because he had to save and pay off the debt back home and send money for the family to live on. Furthermore, he wanted to buy a house for when he brought his family over to the UK, which was a huge task. He always accepted overtime work at the factory and worked six days a week like many of his countrymen to earn more money. They all counted the pounds in rupees which would go a long way in India, sufficient for the families to have an excellent quality of life and enough left to pay towards their debts. Bashir managed to pay the debt within a year and concentrated on saving money to buy a house and on airfares for the family, which would take some time. Also, the family back home reclaimed the land from the landlords from whom Bashir had borrowed some money to pay for his journey to the UK and, with the land back in their possession, Bashir's parents were able to farm again with the help of Bashir's brother so, as for the others, it was all looking good for Bashir and he became more confident.

Back at home, once Amina had received some money from Bashir, she told the family that they would not have to worry for the next three months as there was enough to buy good quality food and some clothes for the winter. They were also happy that Bashir had found a job and settled down with a good quality of life for himself in the UK, whilst Amina became more confident and reassured the family that they would not have to suffer any more and would be joining Bashir shortly. Amina played her part in managing the family finances and taking care of the children and her in-laws. Bashir at the same time was content with being in the UK and started thinking ahead to the time when he could invite the family to join him. To do that, however he must save money and work hard for as many hours as possible, eat healthily and buy a house. So, he did not spend money on himself apart from going to the movies and buying a few cheap fashionable "made in Britain" clothes from the market which he wore proudly and made him feel part of being in Britain.

Bashir started visiting his friends from other towns and cities such as Blackburn and Leicester where Gujarati Indians were settling. He was impressed by how the roads and motorways and countryside were so clean and how people obeyed the driving laws. It allowed him to see the pleasant side of Britain with long summer months lots of greenery. The only thing the Asians did not understand was why the flowers in the parks and gardens did not have much of a scent, whereas back at home you could smell them as you walked past them. Those who settled with their families also helped others morally and financially, and Bashir got many offers of money to help bring over his family when he visited his fellow countrymen. There was a sense of growing community spirit in these places, which was reassuring not only to Bashir but to others who were in a similar situation. Then there came a time when he put aside some money for new fashionable clothes and went to town, taking Salim, who was aged fourteen and lived in the same neighbourhood, with him. Salim had been in the UK for two years and could speak English fairly well. He would often assist people by taking them to a shop in town and interpreting so that they could have a suit tailor- made for themselves.

Bashir had been longing for this ever since he saw the photographs of Ismail and his friends in suits and ties, which their families had displayed back at home. They found a shop that was immensely popular amongst Asians, and he asked Salim to interpret for him. Bashir told the tailor that he wanted a dark grey Italian- style mohair suit, because by working in the textile mill, he had learnt about different types of cloth. The tailor measured him and asked them to return in three weeks to collect the suit. Afterwards, they went to another men's shop to buy a shirt, tie, shoes, and matching socks. Although his money was tight, he just managed to pay for them all. Three weeks later, going to collect the suit, Bashir wore the new shirt, tie and shoes and armed with a contemporary portable radio which he borrowed from a friend, he headed towards the town. He had also grown a moustache and was clean-shaven with

From the Splendid Sun to the Glorious Pound

stylish jet-black hair. Bashir tried on the suit and looked in the mirror and was very impressed. He asked Salim to thank the tailor. He wore the suit and put his old clothes in a bag and came out in a joyful mood. He proclaimed to Salim that he was almost an English gentleman. He told Salim to take him to a photographer's shop in a nearby street. Here Bashir asked Salim to explain to the photographer how he wanted the photograph to be taken and, as the photographer was already familiar with how the Asians regularly had photographs taken, there was not much of a problem. The photographer made him comfortable but, because Bashir had never had a photograph taken apart from the passport photographs taken back home, he was a bit nervous. So, as directed by the photographer Bashir sat up straight, looking at the camera, holding the portable radio looking very relaxed and content with the whole set-up. He felt proud of what he had achieved and of the fact that he was well on his way to becoming a respectable British citizen. He could not wait to send the photographs to Amina.

The next day, a Sunday morning as Bashir was on his way to the cinema as the Asians did almost every Sunday, he came across a church. The bells were ringing, and he saw some white people on their way into the church. Bashir thought to himself that these Christians were more religious than he and other Muslims who hardly ever prayed five times a day which they should have been doing. He was even more surprised to see how the churchgoers were dressed for the occasion – men in suits with hats and women dressed in long dresses covering their entire bodies and hats. This was something to consider for Bashir and made him think deeply with a sort of guilty feeling that God had listened to his prayers and granted a new life for him and his family, so he asked himself how he might have forgotten to pray daily and not be thankful for his achievements. In the evening Bashir and his friends were sitting around the fireplace whilst waiting for the food to be cooked: beef curry, pilau rice and carrot halwa, real delicacies when everyone was at home on Saturday evening. It was customary to sit around the fireplace in a group and talk about movies, work, families, and friendship. Their life revolved around waking up to go to work and then go home eat and sleep.

Bashir briefly narrated the story about seeing the white churchgoers to his fellow tenants, which led them to display similar feelings of guilt. Since everyone had the same things

From the Splendid Sun to the Glorious Pound

in common, there were no fallouts, and it was all a feel-good factor for them. Abdul was going to buy a house, so they had all agreed to lend him some money and to ask other friends in the neighbourhood to raise further finance because the concept of buying with a mortgage and paying interest was not considered appropriate Islamically. This was the normal procedure amongst the Muslim immigrants and Bashir was reassured that once he was ready to invite his family, he also would be supported in the same way.

CHAPTER FOUR

New Life, New Way

Bashir got used to being in the UK and was doing well in the factory. The only downside was not being able to communicate with his family, apart from their monthly letters. When he received the letter from his wife after she had seen his photographs, she joked that he should not get used to being alone. However, the family were happy to see him looking healthy and gaining weight, an indication of his prosperity. He was slowly recovering from the initial culture shock of being here and occasionally working long hours, sometimes almost seven days a week in the factory during the dark winter months. Now he was enjoying the summer with all its blossom. It was a breath of fresh air for him. He would visit the countryside in Yorkshire with his friends, and the farms were a reminder of working on the farms back home but, he knew he would rather work in the factory and earn wages in pounds rather than a few rupees. It was six months since he had started work and he was now able to work with speed, and with overtime his salary had increased. Bashir had settled well and within a year he managed to pay all the debt he had amassed in India. His next plans were to buy a house and bring his family to the UK. By this time, more migrants had started arriving from India and Pakistan and a small community was being established. Although the Indians would go back home to visit families and return after a few weeks, the majority remained in the UK preoccupied with making long- term plans. Whereas, for the Pakistanis, who mostly originated from Kashmir in Pakistan, the thought of settling with their families in the UK did not attract them simply because their loyalties remained with Pakistan, and some were contemplating returning and investing money in farms and businesses. The main reason for this was that very few Pakistanis had a history of migrating overseas and this was their first experience of coming to the UK.

The Indians in the UK had the advantage of having role models such as the Indians who had settled in Africa with their families many years ago, built up a good quality of life and never returned to India. They were segregated by their skin colour and culture. In the beginning they were farmers, contracted labourers, government officials, and later started investing in businesses in East Africa. So, it was these

New Life, New Way

business opportunities that attracted the Indians to settle in East Africa. They realised that there was a market available, so they established shops throughout East Africa, starting on the coast and later moving inland. Although the Indians in the UK were not professionals, they did not have to struggle like Indians in Africa as the UK gave them employment, full rights such as British citizenship, voting rights, free education, and health care, and they were free to form their own spaces for identity and community.

At last Amina and her family back home were enjoying a good quality of life. They could afford good food and clothes, and the roof and the cracks in the house walls had been repaired, thanks to Bashir and the UK. Bashir too was enjoying himself here and went on a day trip to Blackpool organised by their employer, on a coach full of fellow factory workers. It reminded the Asians of the open spaces with fresh air that they were used to back home when they would go for a day out with the whole family to a fairground a few miles away from their villages, where the children would enjoy simple rides and the whole family would enjoy the street foods, various entertainments from magicians and acrobatic displays. Afterwards they would go back home to

From the Splendid Sun to the Glorious Pound

drop off their wives and small children who stayed at home. Then the men along with the grown-up children would return to the same fairground.

Later in the evening, the rides and the daytime entertainment were shut down and, instead, a stage was erected, and hundreds of people gathered seated on the floor in an open space and would stay there till morning listening to Qawwali concerts till morning (a style of Muslim devotional poetic song and music associated with Sufis). A Qawwali group normally consisted of the lead singer, singing poetry, romantic and religious songs along with the chorus, and playing a variety of musical instruments as the audience became mesmerised, and some even got lost in a trance. The youngsters would become a little too excited, sometimes leading to disturbances and a brawl or two between two opposing groups.

In Blackpool on the Pleasure Beach there was one of the world's most ride-intensive amusement parks with adrenaline-fuelled adventure and thrills. Bashir and his Asian fellow workers enjoyed themselves on the beach eating the food they brought from home as there was no halal food available here. Their white fellow workers were enjoying the

New Life, New Way

beers, fish and chips and sunbathing, Bashir and a number of the others had some photographs taken to send back home. It was traditional all over the UK to go for a day trip from their workplaces in summer and on the whole, all the workers had a brilliant time in Blackpool. On the way back the coach stopped at a pub just before reaching home and most of their white workmates got off to have some drinks whilst Bashir and his Asian friends stayed on the coach, although one or two Asians who used to drink alcohol slipped through the net and went to the pub as well. After one or two drinks, their workmates returned to the coach and because some of them had already had some drinks in Blackpool they were a bit tipsy (a British slang expression for slightly drunk) they were full of humour and made everyone laugh. Most Asians were by now getting used to seeing aspects of British culture and had drawn clear distinctions between the two cultures, and their white workmates had grown to respect the Muslims, who were more determined to maintain their own cultural and religious identities.

Within six months, Ismail had bought a small house and so Bashir moved in with him. By that time more migrants were coming to the UK from Gujarat, and they needed somewhere to stay, and so landlords such as Ismail would accommodate them. It worked in perfect harmony because the migrants not only had places to stay but would also get support from the others who would guide them while they settled down here, buy food in bulk and save money all round. The landlords would receive rent which not only paid the domestic bills but went towards the cost of bringing their families over here. Although the new migrants were facing overcrowding (as many as four to ten people in a house), they were not able to socialise with the white community simply because of the language and cultural barriers. They also did not have the spare time to venture outside their growing community life and so they thought that the best way to survive was to recreate the village type of life here, which gave them comfort and security.

It was two years since Bashir had arrived in the UK. He had bought a small house with some of his savings and some money borrowed from his friends. The day came when he moved into his own house and, like Ismail, accommodated four tenants which gave him extra income to pay for his family to join him. After four months his family obtained passports and visas and prepared to sail for the

New Life, New Way

UK. They were travelling by ship because it was a lot cheaper than the plane and they were allowed to bring more pieces of luggage, enabling them to buy lots of necessary household goods before they left India. Amina and the two children made their preparations and started shopping from the lists Bashir had sent them, which included Indian goods that were much cheaper than in the UK such as cotton bedding, handmade blankets, and pots and pans particularly useful for Indian cooking which they did not even sell in the UK. Amina also bought dresses for herself and her daughter because traditional Indian clothes were not available here, whereas the boys did not have any problems with wearing English clothes.

In the meantime, things were going smoothly at the factory where Bashir was working, apart from a few teething problems because some Asians had to accept lower-paid manual work compared to the white workers even though some of them were better educated and were able to speak reasonable English. They had no other choice other than to migrate to the UK because, even being educated it would not have been possible to get jobs back home even if they did it would not be sufficient to provide good quality of lifelike in

From the Splendid Sun to the Glorious Pound

the UK. The management at the factory treated the Asian workers well but there was one supervisor who treated the Asian workers in his department with contempt and behaved like a dictator. One day, an argument developed between this supervisor and an educated Pakistani worker who confronted him about the Union laws. The supervisor sacked him on the spot. This sent a shockwave through the Asian workforce (both Indian and Pakistani) and so they waited for the night shift workers to arrive so they too could participate and then held a meeting after work outside the premises.

The white workers were also invited and, although some did sympathise with them, they refused to be drawn into such a conflict because they were treated more favourably with promotions as well as having the privilege of working with superior, modern types of machinery. The Textile Union representative who was supposed to protect the rights of the workers was hesitant about protecting the rights of the Asian workers and took the side of the management. Interestingly, although the phrase "working class" was used by the historians and social scientists of the time, they were in fact referring to the "white working class" with this definition. The Asian or the Black working classes were instead referred to as immigrants and this gave the lie to the idea that, in the UK, the "working class" also included multiracial and multi-cultural communities. The Asians had heard of the treatment of Indian workers by the British Colonials back home, but never envisaged that the day would come when they would have to face such humiliation here. The notion of sticking together to support their fellow brothers came back to them and emotions ran high as they felt no matter what might happen, they would not back down. They appointed Ayub, an educated Indian worker who was fluent in English as their leader and he agreed to represent them. He told them to continue with work the next day, so they all went to work as they normally did, apart from the worker who had been sacked who stayed at home. Ayub had a meeting with the manager, and, after a long discussion, they failed to reach an agreement. As soon as he informed the Asian workers of the result of the meeting, they unanimously agreed to go on strike. They stopped working straight away and walked out.

The management took the side of the supervisor fearing that if they reinstated the workers, it would look as though they had given in to their demands and would set a precedence for future strikes. The next day, Ayub gathered the workers outside the factory and the manager came out and excused them for having an illegal strike without the approval of the Textile Union. The workers kept chanting that they wanted equal rights, but the manager stood there and remained firm. Finally, Ayub had no choice and with great sadness, he had to tell the workers to go home, but whilst he was talking, one Indian worker told him to stop for a moment and walked toward the manager. He could not hide his emotion and although he could not speak English, he asked the manager in Gujarati, "Mr Parkin to you, your supervisor is a human and so are we donkeys? This speech was translated by Ayub in English for the manager, who nevertheless stuck to his decision and so that was the end of the meeting and they all walked away. It was not a pleasant experience for them because when they had initially arrived in the UK, life seemed better than they could have hoped for, and they were not expecting anything like this to happen. It was the biggest blow that could have happened to them, and they felt that their livelihood and any dreams of having a better future with their families were shattered.

However, when other Asians in the community heard about this, many volunteered to help them with money and by finding jobs through their network of people who worked in other factories. It was quite normal for Asian workers to get help when they encountered problems with low wages and exploitation in factories. Bashir and the others also registered themselves with the Employment Exchange in town, which gave them unemployment benefits and helped them to find jobs. This was a great relief and Bashir was pleasantly surprised as he did not expect the government to provide these kinds of services. Back home if there were droughts or the business was not doing well, the whole family became victims of poverty with no support from the government because the economy was still declining. Bashir did not feel the need to inform Amina because he did not want to upset her and advised her to continue with the plans for coming to the UK. There were many textile factories within a range of about eight miles and with their experience they all got employment either through friends or the Employment Exchange. They suffered from a bit of financial hardship for a brief time, but they grew more confident and continued with their dreams and ambitions.

From the Splendid Sun to the Glorious Pound

Bashir got a job as a machine operator and was earning a bit more than from the previous job, so they were back on track to embark on their journey. For Bashir and the others there was no looking back, and any obstacles and mistakes were a learning process and a small price to pay. Amina continued with the plans to leave for the UK and finally, they had a date to sail. They were leaving on a ship within two weeks.

This time they did not have to travel discreetly like Bashir, and they started visiting the extended family and villagers to say farewell, which was customary before leaving for abroad, as they were not sure when they would return. These were very emotional moments, but reassuring too as the villagers, particularly the elderly, blessed them with prayers and good wishes. After two weeks as planned, the family left, and the neighbours and extended family members walked with them to the main road where a bullock cart was waiting to take them to the railway station from where Bashir had started his train journey to Bombay. The grandparents were the last to hug the family and they all burst into tears, which was a tradition amongst the villagers because of being such a close-knit community. Like Bashir, Amina and the two children had a last look at the village as they set off for the

New Life, New Way

train station. Bashir's brother and sister-in-law were to accompany them to Bombay. They all had similar experiences to that of Bashir on the train journey, enjoying the scenery and seeing happy, smiling passengers. Once at Bombay station they were met by a representative from the travel agent called Amoji who took them to a guest house. The next day they enjoyed some sightseeing and the different food. They too bought some warm clothes but, unlike Bashir, they did not have to buy from the flea market. Instead, they bought new and fashionable clothes because Bashir had already sent some money in advance.

Back in the UK Bashir was preoccupied with organising the house. He bought items of furniture from the second-hand shops and worked extra hours at the factory to earn more money to spend when the whole family was finally reunited. With such a feel-good factor in his life, he did not care much about going to the cinema and restaurants. Ismail and his friends helped him to decorate the house and Bashir stocked up with all the household necessities to welcome the family. In Bombay, Amina and the children were about to board the ship and Amoji and Bashir's brother and sister-in-law accompanied them and cleared them through the

From the Splendid Sun to the Glorious Pound

immigration services before they headed towards the ship. Since Bashir could only afford to pay for the cheapest fare, they were directed to the lower deck by the crew members who showed them to their cabin, with the hundreds of other hopeful Indians boarding the ship sailing to the UK towards a better future. After an emotional final farewell, Amoji and Bashir's brother and sister-in-law left. Later, Amina and the children were on the deck amongst hundreds of passengers waving goodbye to relatives and friends who were waving back with handkerchiefs. As the ship set sail, Bombay got further and further away and slowly started disappearing into the distance until the passengers could not see it anymore.

They remained on the top deck; the sea was calm and there were many chairs where they sat and enjoyed the ice cream and cold drinks being served all-inclusive in the fare. This was enjoyable for the whole family although they were a little sad and started feeling a bit uncomfortable. Later on, they went back to their cabin and were served some tea, biscuits and fruit and they all relaxed more. Ahmed had a nap on the top bunk, whereas Amina and Jameela slept on the bottom bunks. When they got up, the children started looking through the cabin porthole and enjoyed the panoramic views of the sea which was just as well because they found the ship a bit claustrophobic as they had been brought up in the open space of the village. Later, they all went to the restaurant upstairs and sat down to eat with other passengers, mostly Indians from different castes and backgrounds, but here they had one thing in common. They were going to be sailing to the UK for over two weeks together so getting to know each other was especially important. Most of the white passengers were travelling from Australia and were enjoying the food. For the Indians, however, the English food was a bit bland which they were not used to, and there were no catering facilities for Indian food, so they had to make do with bread, rice, and some vegetable soup, not an ideal option.

After two days the ship approached Aden and they could see the city. It was customary for the passengers to visit Aden and buy presents, but they had to get into small boats to sail into the city because the water was too shallow for the ship to dock. The main attractions were wrist watches because they were cheaper than in the UK and so Amina bought a watch for each of them and one for Bashir. Then they returned to the ship and continued the journey. On the

From the Splendid Sun to the Glorious Pound

top deck, the passengers relaxed looking at the sea. Whilst Europeans were sunbathing, rubbing sun cream on their bodies, which the Indians found a bit strange because they had no knowledge of people with white skin are prone to get sunburnt and must use sun cream to protect themselves. The Europeans, including a few Hindus, drank alcohol whereas most Indians sat in a larger group chitchatting and enjoying ice cream and snacks such as Bombay mix snack (which consists of a variable mixture of spicy, dried ingredients, such as fried lentils, peanuts, chickpeas, corn, puffed rice and fried onions) which they brought with them. Overall, it was a colourful, cheerful atmosphere where the children would play games and it became the daily routine. One fly in the ointment was that Amina and a few of the first-time travellers started feeling seasick and, not being able to eat properly, their health declined. The children, however, were fine as they were using their energies by being active and playing games.

A few days more and they were approaching the Suez Canal and they had to wait for hours before the ship was able to sail through it. Suddenly local Arab traders started coming out to them in small boats and some climbed onto the ship displaying their market style goods. They would shout the names of the Indian Prime Minister Nehru, and the Egyptian President Nasser, because he had helped India by blocking the Suez Canal to prevent the Portuguese government sending its army to India to defend its colony Goa from India who captured Goa in 1962 and with the support of President Nasser, Goa became an integral part of India. As the ship started sailing very slowly through the canal, people were buying dazzling white shirts nicely presented in cellophane packets, middle eastern ornaments and toys. The customers had to haggle for the cheapest prices which the Indians were used to doing back home. Many of the passengers were Gujaratis who are traditionally known for being careful with their money and, anyway, they only had limited amounts of cash, so they could barely afford to buy these goods. The Arabs sold more to the tourists and the majority of European passengers. Also, there was some work going on in the Suez Canal and the passengers would entertain themselves by joking with the workers, as the ship sailed slowly by.

Soon, the Arab traders left the ship, and the ship was sailing into the open sea again where the passengers went back to their routine shipboard activities. The children too had made some friends and were having fun, apart from missing the Indian food. They were enjoying being on the ship and were even able to talk to some of the crew members who were from Daman district in Gujarat, and so were speaking in Gujarati to the children. In some respects, it was educational for the children because they would ask the crew members questions about the different countries, they were sailing past and the names of different fish in the sea. The majority of the children had never been to cinemas back home and were having their first taste of movies starring Charlie Chaplin or Laurel and Hardy, which did not require much knowledge of English to understand, and they found them very funny. In particular, the police wearing tall helmets chasing the villains with truncheons which reminded them of the times when their parents or neighbours used to chase them across the open space in their villages for causing mischief. They also watched detective movies and documentaries about life in the UK and, because the white people (mainly the elderly) took a liking to these youngsters, they were given sweets and chocolates. For the youngsters, this was their first experience of socialising with white

New Life, New Way

people and because the youngsters learned some keywords in English, they were able to interact with them.

Ahmed and his friend would go into the open pub on the top deck and smiled at the European passengers. They would go to the corner where there was a piano and tried to mimic the Qawwali songs and play the piano in the way Ahmed remembered from the time when he used to go with his dad in India to listen to the Qawwali. Ahmed and his friend were quite loud but the people in the pub just politely told them to keep the noise down. Ahmed and his friend were a bit curious about the different colours of the drinks in the pub and one day they spoke to the English barman. Ahmed pointed towards the different colours of drinks which the adults were being served. They had mistaken the drinks for non-alcoholic Indian sherbet drinks and asked to be served. The barman tried to explain that it was forbidden for children of their age because it was alcohol, but Ahmed and his friend did not understand, so the man acted like a drunk and Ahmed and his friend got the message and left laughing. Although Amina and a few others were still being seasick it did not affect their desire and determination to settle in the UK and, although Muslim women do not normally dance

From the Splendid Sun to the Glorious Pound

because it is against their religion, she was enjoying herself with other Indian families as they sat in a large group in a hall whilst some of the Hindu ladies put on colourful Indian saris (a length of cloth worn by Indian women, wrapping themselves in silk, cotton or linen) and performed traditional festive dances or danced to Indian movie songs.

In the meantime, back in the UK, Bashir was counting the days and had already booked a week's holiday to spend with his family. The Indian grocery shop was owned by his cousin Riaz, who helped him out by selling him some groceries at cost price and gave him extra items for free. The remaining, Bashir did not have to pay for until next month. His tenants had already moved out and Bashir had the house to himself, so he was able to organise it for the family's arrival.

The ship had reached the port of Marseille in France. By that time, the sea was very rough, and the passengers could not go on to the top deck anymore because of the huge waves and so had to stay on the lower decks. The Indian passengers started to get a taste of the cold and windy weather. There were few people to greet the passengers and the port was quiet, dull and wet. The ship soon started

New Life, New Way

sailing towards London. Amina and the children were excited and started packing the luggage and exchanging contact details with other passengers. The sea was no longer a clear blue or green as it had been earlier in the journey but was now brown under a stormy and windy sky as the ship headed towards the UK. Finally, the ship arrived at Tilbury docks. All the passengers were ready and waiting as the ship was crowded with relatives and friends, shaking hands with each other, and excitedly exchanging hugs. Bashir was worried seeing Amina had lost some weight and looked ill, but Amina told him whilst hugging him that this was the least of her worries and, for her, the family being united was the most fulfilling outcome. Here there was no excitement of seeing people welcoming them with waving handkerchiefs as it would have been in India.

After collecting the hand luggage, Bashir arranged for the remaining pieces of luggage to be delivered to their home. Then they disembarked and, after going through customs, walked towards a minibus where the driver who normally took Bashir and the other workers to work was waiting, as it was cheaper than the train. To the relief of Amina and the children, the driver kept the minibus warm and, before

From the Splendid Sun to the Glorious Pound

setting off, Bashir gave them some food which included chicken masala, some samosas which Bashir had cooked and warm masala tea in thermos flasks. Amina, although a bit shy in front of the driver, could not resist asking Bashir where he had bought this food. Bashir smiled and told her that there were no restaurants or takeaways, so he had cooked it himself which Amina and the children found surprising and hilarious because, back at home, husbands did not normally cook. The wives would not allow it because traditionally it was their duty. They headed for Dewsbury and Amina and the children were so tired, that they fell asleep as they were passing along the country roads. After about one hour they were on the M1 motorway travelling at high speed. The minibus headlights lit up the cats' eyes on the motorway in red and yellow colours, which Amina and the children found amazing, together with the width of the road and the open space. In India roads are narrow and travel at night is particularly hazardous as heavy traffic is normal and includes overloaded buses, trucks, scooters, and roaming livestock, all without consideration for the rules of the road, so accidents are quite common. When they reached the halfway point, they pulled up at a motorway service station to refuel and to use the toilets. Bashir took the family inside and Amina and the children found the place with shops remarkably interesting.

The driver treated them to some coffee, biscuits, some chocolate and crisps and the children were very excited because they had never had such treats which were only available in big cities back home due to poverty. After about two hours, they reached Dewsbury and parked outside their house, which Ismail had been keeping warm and was waiting for them. Once they were all inside, Bashir made them comfortable, and Ismail took out some biryani which he had prepared along with some Lassi yoghurt drink. After freshening up, they ate the food which Amina and the children enjoyed very much, although Amina did not overindulge, fearing that not having had spicy food for over two weeks, she might get an upset stomach. The driver and Ismail left, and the family was ready for bed, so Bashir showed them around the house and where the outside toilet was.

From the Splendid Sun to the Glorious Pound

Chapter Five

New Dawn, New Hope

The next morning the family got up and Bashir talked them through all the facilities in the house and for Amina and the children, it was not much of an issue as they were used to using an English bathroom on the ship, whereas here using basic facilities like an outside toilet and in the cellar a basic cubicle with a boiler and a bucket for having a shower was a bit of a climb- down compared to when they were on the ship. As the family were getting ready for breakfast Bashir looked at Amina smiling. He told the family that he was going to make breakfast and jokingly implied that since he had almost become an Englishman it was going to be an English breakfast. The children looked a bit puzzled because they had seen enough English food on the ship but Amina smiled and didn't say anything and in a happy mood started helping him to cook, but Bashir surprised her and started cooking some Indian omelettes knowing that Amina and the children must have missed them and he told Amina to make some Indian masala tea (spicy tea) which she used to make back at home because he

From the Splendid Sun to the Glorious Pound

had missed it a lot. Finally, they sat down to eat the breakfast and their new family life began.

After breakfast, they all freshened up, put on the warm clothes Bashir had bought for them and were ready to meet friends and relatives who would come to see them later. The family sat down to sort out the luggage which consisted of clothes and other personal belongings whilst the children were tucking into chocolates, sweets, cakes, and crisps that Bashir had bought for them and placed on a table. Bashir asked about the family and friends back at home and got to know how things had been since he had left the village. Amina told him that the extended family was doing well and many more from the village were queuing to come over to the UK. Whilst they were talking there was a knock on the door and, when Bashir opened it, he saw that it was a couple from the neighbourhood, Rafiq, and Ruksana, with two children holding boxes. They had come to meet Amina and the children, and they entered the house and put the boxes on the table. For the last two years, many families from Gujarat had settled here and were eager to meet newly arrived families.

Amina was happy to meet them because she had already

heard about them from Bashir on the way from the docks. Bashir introduced the family to Amina and the children, and Ruksana informed them that the boxes contained some food that she had cooked, which Bashir and Amina appreciated. It was customary to bring Mithai (Indian sweets) but there were no shops here that sold it, so they brought cake instead which the children loved because they had got used to eating it on the ship. The socialisation process had begun and whilst Bashir and Rafiq talked about their work, his wife Ruksana informed Amina that life for Indian women was a lot different here compared to life in a village. Here they had to get used to a different routine, she said, and told Amina about the social isolation due to not having many cultural activities and open spaces like back home. Apart from shopping and taking the children to school the majority were stay-at-homes. Amina saw them looking healthy, prosperous, and happy, which reassured her, and soon they sat down to eat the food which Ruksana had brought, and the children tucked into the cakes.

The next morning Riaz the shopkeeper dressed in a long khaki work coat came to meet Amina and the children. He was a charismatic figure and asked them if they wanted any help and money even though he had already stocked up on all the necessary groceries for the family from his shop. As the days went by, more visitors came to meet them and brought food to eat with them. Bashir spent most of the time briefing Amina and the kids about the weekly routines such as the chicken man bringing live chickens, the milkman, the dustbin men, and the monthly delivery of coal. Bashir's English was still not that good so, after a week, he asked Riaz for help to get Amina and the children registered at the doctor's surgery and to enrol Ahmed and Jameel at the schools. A couple of days later, Bashir took Amina and the children to town and bought some warm clothes, and they too experienced, as Bashir had, seeing the Christmas lights and other festive activities and enjoyed the friendly behaviour of the white people. Bashir had two weeks' holiday from work and so was able to spend quality time with the family. They went for meals at friends' houses which gave Amina and the children some idea of the lifestyles of people from diverse backgrounds.

A week later the remaining luggage had arrived which consisted of household goods and some Indian pickles. They unpacked bedding, such as woollen blankets woven by

New Dawn, New Hope

hand by sheep merchants which were normally used in Indian villages because of the pure, authentic lamb wool which would keep them warm in winter, with cotton- filled pillows and handmade quilts, which are ethically made by traditional craftspeople, are environmentally friendly and machine washable. Also, a pestle and mortar, traditionally used to prepare ingredients or substances by crushing and grinding them into a fine paste or powder in the kitchen, together with a butchers' block made from a tree stump, usually from the Neem tree, and used for chopping meat.

There were several types of home-grown organic rice and Jowar flour (commonly called Sorghum flour) and used to make jowar roti (thick chapattis), which the villagers ate daily at breakfast. Buffalo ghee (ghee is a type of clarified butter made from the milk of buffalo or cow, used in cooking in the Indian subcontinent) would be spread on the jowar roti and this would then be eaten with a good dollop of buffalo cream and a warm cup of Masala tea. Different types of home-grown, organic daal (lentils) commonly used in the cuisine in the Indian subcontinent, were among the goods which were not available in the UK, would last for a few years and would save money. Soon, Bashir went back to work and the children started school after three weeks, so Amina would pack lunches for Bashir and the children and then remain at home carrying out the domestic tasks and getting used to the daily routines. His workmates at the factory congratulated Bashir for being reunited with his family. Ahmed started attending the all-boys secondary modern school and he was welcomed by the headmaster. Ahmed was placed in a class full of white pupils apart from one Pakistani named Arif, so Ahmed sat next to him so they both felt comfortable. The teacher and white pupils were communicating in English which Ahmed and Arif were unable to understand so they felt frustrated and isolated and just sat there like dummies.

This lasted for a month, but as more Asian pupils started attending the school as they started to arrive from Indian villages back home, the situation became critical. Now there were about fourteen of them. After consulting the teachers, the headmaster decided to create a special class for these pupils and to teach them English at levels that were common for an equivalent six-year-old native. The classroom was located outside the main building and classes would begin with lessons on the alphabet, then the children read simple

New Dawn, New Hope

books consisting of pictures and drawings. The pupils had to get used to being like small children learning the basic lessons of different topics. The Asian students were also taken to the town, market, parks, and other places of interest so that they would have some understanding of the British way of life and on their return, they would have group discussions and learn the English words to identify what they had seen whilst out visiting places.

The classes were informal. The teachers spoke slowly to the pupils in a way that they would find easier to understand the lesson content. Quite often the other pupils and teachers had laughed when the Asian pupils were reading funny stories in books. As far as the dinner was concerned the Asians were unwilling to eat the bland English dishes in the canteen, instead, they opted for Asian food and like their fathers who took food from home to the factories, the children brought packed lunches and in the morning they placed the food on the radiators in the classroom so that it would remain warm for them to eat at lunch break in the classroom, sharing the different home-cooked food and chatting away amongst themselves having fun, whilst the white pupils would eat food freshly cooked for them in the canteen. When the teacher came into the special classroom after lunch break the whole room would smell of spicy food which the teacher did not mind because the pupils made sure that the place was very tidy.

The Asian pupils were caught in two cultures: the body language and speaking were so different in England compared to back home in India and Pakistan and so there was a lot of confusion. The teachers had a difficult task in disciplining these children, particularly when they were told to speak in English amongst themselves, even in broken English so that at least they would get used to learning to communicate in English, but they found it very difficult to comply with that and kept speaking in Urdu and Gujarati because, like their parents, they were not feeling part of the British way of life. On Sunday they would go to the cinemas like their dads and uncles which was free for schoolchildren, so when they came to school on Monday, they came wearing colourful fashionable clothes (as there were no school uniform requirements) and different hairstyles like their Indian movie heroes. They would sing or deliver dialogues from the movies and would even try to act like the characters in the movies. So, talking in English amongst themselves was out of the question and when the teacher asked them to talk in English, they started narrating the stories of the movies, which the teacher did not mind as long as they tried to speak in English, and it was all fun. In the morning they would join the white pupils in the morning assembly and when the Christian hymns were sung, the Muslim children would recite Islamic prayers quietly.

Afterwards, the pupils were given a free bottle of milk and they would buy crisps and wafer biscuits called Wagon Wheels, which the Asians found very tasty - not knowing Wagon Wheels are made with beef gelatine which was haram (forbidden) for them. They also witnessed the commemoration of the First World War and, although the Asian pupils had no idea what this event was about, they participated in the events as taught by their teachers and wore the red poppy. Later, as they studied further the history of both world wars, they began to realise the devastation Germany, Italy and Japan had caused and how the First and the Second World Wars were won by the allies. However, what they were not told was that British historians did not write about the more than a million Indian soldiers who served in WW1 as a part of the British Indian Army or the more than 74,000 who died in the conflict. In WW2, over 87,000 Indian soldiers (including those from modern day Pakistan, Bangladesh, and the Nepalese Ghurkhas) and three million civilians died.

Until now they had only known of the time back home when they used to celebrate the nation's independence from the British rulers on 15 August 1947. On this occasion, the school, the pupils (Hindus and Muslims) would get up early in the morning, dress smartly and help each other to make flower garlands, balloons, and other decorative materials to create colourful decorations in the yard outside the school. They would sing the national anthem with patriotic speeches and songs by students, and speeches delivered by the teacher to make the pupils aware of the sacrifices people had to make to gain independence from the British rulers. Afterwards, the teachers and pupils would walk to the small, close-knit community two miles away from the village where the untouchables lived. This was an annual ritual because Gandhi believed that the untouchables should be respected and did not approve of the Hindus from higher castes discriminating against the untouchables and regarding them as inferior. The untouchables would welcome the teachers

New Dawn, New Hope

and sit with the pupils on the ground in the courtyard. Mahatma Gandhi once said that "Untouchability is a soul-destroying sin, and the caste system is a social evil. Gandhi instilled into the Hindus that the lower caste Hindus have been suppressed and regarded as "Untouchable" as inferiors to the higher castes and so they had to be removed and should be given equal rights in education, and government departments and they must be treated with respect.

Similarly, the Pakistani students also remembered their Independence Day observed annually in Pakistan on 14 August 1947, which is a national holiday in Pakistan. It commemorates the day when Pakistan achieved independence from its British rulers and was declared a sovereign state which came into existence as a result of the Pakistan movement, which aimed at the creation of an independent Muslim state via partition. The movement was led by the All-India Muslim League under the leadership of Muhammad Ali Jinnah. Independence comprised West Pakistan (present-day Pakistan) and East Pakistan (now Bangladesh). Nowadays the main Independence Day ceremony takes place in Islamabad, where the national flag is hoisted on the Presidential and Parliament buildings. It is

From the Splendid Sun to the Glorious Pound

followed by the national anthem and live televised speeches by leaders. Usual celebratory events and festivities for the day include flag-raising ceremonies, parades, cultural events, and the playing of patriotic songs. The Gujarati Indians did not continue to celebrate Indian Independence Day in the UK, but the Pakistani leaders here did organise celebrations at the Town Hall, with speeches from community leaders, followed by entertainment by local groups who sang nationalist songs.

School played an especially important part in shaping the future of Asian children, giving them the opportunity to learn about British history which was different from the history of the British Empire which they were familiar with back at home. They learnt about the British culture and the Christian religion, but they were studying separately from the white pupils and interacted only amongst themselves. Even at break time the Asians would gather separately in the playground and might play cricket or just talk among themselves. Some English children did try to socialise with the Asians and exchanged sweets, but the white pupils would also innocently ask questions such as did the Asians put garlic in their hair, because their clothes used to smell of spicy food because they were living in small houses where

New Dawn, New Hope

clothes would be dried in the room next to the kitchen. The white community had not started eating Indian food yet, so the white pupils found it difficult to understand the complex spices and the associated smells of Indian cuisine. The Asians could not understand why, after ruling India for over two hundred years the British had not inherited some of the Indian cultures.

On the other hand, the Asian kids were so happy that they were not beaten in school for being naughty like they would have been back in their countries of origin. They did, however, witness the white pupils being beaten for misbehaving by teachers. The pupil would normally be told to bend over, and the teacher would use a slipper with a worn-out sole and slap him on his backside. In fact, the teacher did not have to beat the Asians because they were mostly well -behaved and the teacher realised that the newly-arrived children would find it traumatic, so the one or two naughty ones were not punished. However, the Asians had their fair share of punishment at the madrasas (religious schools) back home where the Muslim clergy would beat them with a long bamboo stick usually on their hands and sometimes the more angry teachers would even beat them on their back leaving scars in some cases, in which case the teacher had to go through a disciplinary procedure of suspension for a few days without pay, imposed by the madrasa committee, which was all part of the traditions and the parents did not mind. Instead, it was normal for them to inform the teacher if their children misbehaved at home.

For the children in the UK, there were no Madrasa (religious schools) when they first arrived so there was no added pressure and mums would normally teach them at home, so they escaped the harsh punishment of teachers in the event of misbehaving, which was the norm back home. Also, back home if the kids had arguments, scuffled, or had a fallout they may not speak for a few days and were disciplined by parents and teachers. Here, at school English children who had quarrels would go out into a field, the others would follow them, and the two individuals would have aggressive fist fights, then shake hands and go home and next day they would be friends again the Asians found this surprising. Jameela was sent to an all-girls school. There too the Asian children were placed in a special class and had to learn everything from the beginning, just like the boys, and went through similar experiences of eating a home-packed Asian lunch and interacting among themselves in the playground. Those who were a lot younger were placed in state junior schools according to their age and they were better placed to benefit from the schools and did not have to be segregated.

Now six months had passed, and Bashir and Amina and the children had settled well and got used to the routines and the new lifestyle. The parents missed their parents and the members of the extended family, but the children did not have that many problems because they were so preoccupied with schooling and enjoying themselves with their peer groups. They made many friends with similar backgrounds and interests and created a new adventurous life. The climate did affect them, but they were getting used to playing in the snow. On the other hand, their parents were not able to speak to the family back home as there were no phones there, so they were only able to communicate through letters every couple of months, which was frustrating. Gradually, however, they were also getting used to being here and it also helped them to concentrate more on their newly found future.

The children were venturing out and would go into town

at weekends, do the shopping for home as requested by parents and enjoy eating chocolates and sweets with the spending money they got from their parents. They had not had such luxuries in India and Pakistan. They might also go to a funfair in town and enjoy the rides, particularly the bumper cars. Afterwards, they would play games such as throwing wooden balls to topple the targets which were empty tin cans and participants would be rewarded with a coconut if they were successful. This was a more difficult tasks for the locals than for the Asians who were used to throwing stones to bring down fresh mangos from the trees in the fields back home and played village games Gilli-Danda the game requires two sticks; the bigger stick is called Danda and the smaller one is called Gilli at the raised end both tools were made of wood, which flips into the air and while it is in the air the player strikes the Gilli hitting it as far as possible more like a cricket ball.

Also, Goli Marble games where the player would hit the selected Goli with another Goli that belongs to him, because of such skills the Asian children were experts in hitting targets and the onlookers at the funfair mostly white people, found it very entertaining and the Asian boys were laughing

New Dawn, New Hope

and jumping with joy, speaking in English then suddenly in an Asian language because they could not translate the village jokes into English. The English parents would give the Asians some money to win some coconuts for their children, so finally, the owner would get fed up because they did not miss a single target and won so many coconuts that he ran out of them. Although most English youths also found this entertaining, a couple of others got jealous and nasty and went after the Asian youngsters and tried to chase them from the fairground. The Asian children ran towards the crowd in the fair and sought protection from the owners of the rides.

On Saturday afternoons, the tradition of watching wrestling continued and Bashir and his family would go to friends' houses to watch it, whilst the women would cook food. The children joined their fathers to watch, but they mostly enjoyed watching their dads' adrenaline-filled behaviour as they supported the different wrestlers and made bodily and facial gestures with loud noises. Overall, it was full of fun and with the food on the table it made an excellent party for everyone. Later, the children tried to imitate what they had seen on the TV by wrestling with friends or brothers. On the whole, the family - like other migrants in the UK - started enjoying a happy life. Bashir was the breadwinner and Amina did her duties as a housewife, but without the helpers she would have had back at home where the extended family members would share some of the responsibilities like the communal washing of clothes at the riverside. In fact, this would also have been a social event on sunny days with open space and fresh air.

After Bashir came to the UK, he sent money for Amina to employ a home help, a peasant employed to fetch firewood, clean the kitchen and milk the domestic buffalo and cows which provided milk for the family. Here, Amina cooked and cleaned, although coal for the fire, the groceries, milk, and bread were delivered to their home. On the whole, she was content with living in the UK, but she also felt isolated and stuck at home most of the time, particularly in the winter months, whilst Bashir went to work, and the children attended school. At the weekend they enjoyed being together, going shopping, and visiting friends. As far as halal food was concerned, a farmer would deliver live chickens, normally on Friday or Saturday, and the children would help by holding a live chicken in the kitchen sink which their

New Dawn, New Hope

father would kill according to the Islamic tradition. The children did not mind this as they were brought up seeing such rituals back home. Here the food was plentiful, and they enjoyed family dinners. This new trend of the nuclear family brought them closer and helped them to adopt their new life with harmonious relationships and this paved the way for a better future.

As time went by, more immigrants from India and Pakistan started arriving and so the community started growing. Settled in the UK, they appreciated the British judicial system, the administrative structure, the democracy, and the transport system, particularly the railway networks. These were similar to what the British had introduced in India, the only difference being that, in the Indian subcontinent, the British left the declining economy behind and so, out of desperation, the people in the Indian subcontinent had to resort to corruption and bribery in their administration from the government departments to the civil service and the police. The migrants were seeing on the British news images of more than a million people starving in India due to poverty, the skin on the children's ribs shrivelled and herds of animals with hardly any meat on their bones. When the Indian migrants saw these images, they felt incredibly sad but also appreciated the fact that their future was secured in the UK. The Indians and Pakistanis showed their support which they felt was their duty by sending money to their relatives and friends who were victims of this poverty, and later they would also invite some of them to settle here. As time went by, the lives of the Asians were transformed and were controlled by the rules which were set out following the industrial revolution when Britain was the workshop of the world. The migrants had to adapt to new kinds of behaviour and activities.

The main factor was the time which dictated regimented daily routines, such as waking up, going to work on time and if they were constantly late there was the risk of being sacked. They were also learning to organise their life according to timetables such as for school, keeping appointments, paying domestic bills on time (although that was not much of a problem because the wages were paid on time). It was a much more relaxed lifestyle back home with a siesta in the afternoon followed by teatime with the rest of the family. There was no pressure or controlled behaviour, but the poverty was stifling. The difference between the two ways of life was stark and those who had chosen life in the UK saw it as the best solution.

From the Splendid Sun to the Glorious Pound

CHAPTER SIX

From Injustice to Self-Reliance

It is 1964: two years since Amina and her children arrived. They are settling in well and making lots of friends as more Asians arrive from India and Pakistan and the community becomes larger and more established. The migrants spend most of their time working towards making Britain their home. The menfolk worked in textile factories at unsociable hours, a few worked on three rotating shifts from six in the morning to two in the afternoon, a second week from two to ten in the evening and a third week from ten in the evening to six in the morning. Most of the workers, however, either worked from seven in the evening to seven in the morning or seven in the morning to seven in the evening. Many worked overtime to earn more money because they wanted to move forward with a life of buying better houses and generally improving the quality of life and some wanted to go back home to visit families for about a month at a time. On the whole, they are so busy and preoccupied with family and community life that, despite living in Britain for a few years, they are only able to

From the Splendid Sun to the Glorious Pound

communicate in their mother tongues. They have learned only sufficient English to get them through the work and shopping. They shop at Asian shops, eat Asian food, and socialise among themselves, keeping their cultural traditions alive through an organised community network and co-operation. Although they live in the white working-class areas, they are not able to interact with the white people who socialise at church, in pubs or at the working men's club (members-only clubs run by the workers' unions) so they did not have the opportunity to socialise with the Asians either.

The Asians mostly worked as manual labourers or as machine operators. They were young, with lots of energy and had the experience of working on farms back home which meant that they were fit and healthy, so the work was no problem. The only things they found hard were the wintry weather and the confinement of the enclosed spaces at the factories. The limited family time was also difficult, but they felt that they had come here to earn money no matter how hard they had to work. They valued and admired most of the British education system and continually reminded their children that they had the choice between hard labour, working in factories with oily pieces of machinery, greasy floors and long hours, or a better life through education. So, they advised them, particularly because they did not have to pay fees like back at home, that they must not miss such opportunities to acquire status and not to have to work like them. However, the parents not being able fully to understand the British education system, did not realise how difficult it was for the children who came without any English and who only learned basic English, to progress to further education. Sometimes the schools were unable to help because of the preconceived ideas of a few teachers and careers officers that these children were only good enough to work in factories like their parents. Fathers had to take their sons to work in the factories and most young people worked as labourers. Only a few got better jobs which needed a knowledge of the English language.

As ever more migrants continued to arrive from India and Pakistan, the Asian population kept on rising and many were still living in overcrowded houses and as a close-knit community. This did have lots of social and economic advantages as they all got to know each other, shared common values, got moral and financial support. The womenfolk were bulk buying to save money and benefited

From the Splendid Sun to the Glorious Pound

by socialising with other women, whilst their husbands went to work, and friends continued helping each other to buy houses by lending money. Within four years Bashir bought another house with the money from the sale of the first house and with some savings borrowed from friends and his cousin Riaz. This house had two bedrooms, a bathroom upstairs, a good-sized living room and a small kitchen. Such an achievement was a confidence booster for the whole family. It was quite normal for the migrants to have lodgers, as the landlord would then get extra income from the rent and pay off the debt. So, both lodgers would sleep in a bedroom and Jameela would sleep on a settee in the living room. This lasted for about a year after which the lodgers left as they too bought houses and invited their families over. With such an arrangement, everyone was a winner.

It is 1966: the children have started to become adults and have learned a fair amount of English, so they have started enjoying TV dramas, mainly detective series, and comedies. Bashir has bought a new TV which the whole family enjoy along with a tape recorder. Bashir, like many other Asians can now borrow another tape recorder from friends and copy Indian songs and Qawwali which he and his family

From Injustice to Self-Reliance

used to listen to in India. By now the Asian community is growing and even middle-class and well-to-do young men are coming over from India and Pakistan, some with degrees in law, accountancy and teaching and others as travel agents, railway workers and factory workers.

It is extremely hard for the educated to come to terms with the difficulties of settling in the UK, coming as they did from middle-class backgrounds and straight from colleges and universities but having seen the examples of the immigrants from their villages doing well in the UK, they too want a fair share of the prosperous future here. Amongst the educated ones, are some from poor backgrounds who got places in further education back at home paid for by charities and, later on, friends from the UK sent visas and paid for their flights so that close friends and family members are able to settle here and make a good life for themselves, There were class differences back home so the living standards varied according to their status income, whereas in the UK all the migrants belong to the working-class with similar accommodation and living standards, shared common interests and so they formed groups of small communities in different areas approximately within two to

From the Splendid Sun to the Glorious Pound

three-miles radius so that they are not too far away and could help each other's when needed particularly for the women when the menfolk were working around the clock to earn extra money.

Riaz, Bashir's cousin, who came to Dewsbury in 1954 was very active doing community work as well as running the shop. He would help people to find jobs and continued facilitating those who could not afford to pay cash for groceries, allowing them to pay within a couple of months. He was able to communicate fluently in English, Gujarati, and Urdu and he was instrumental in assisting migrants from India, Pakistan, and East Pakistan (the Bengali Community). He was twenty years old. Before that he was a student in High School and then at a college of further education in India and his parents sent him to a city college in Gujarat, where he studied other languages, apart from his native language Gujarati. He studied Hindi and qualified with a metric certificate which was of a good standard, but it was still difficult to find jobs with as good a wage as in Britain. He came to the UK with a friend, and they were brought to Dewsbury.

He worked in a textile mill in Dewsbury for six months

From Injustice to Self-Reliance

and then worked at another factory that manufactured brakes for automobiles where he was paid more money than the average textile worker. After working for two years, he had saved enough money to start his own bakery business. The parents and community leaders were planning for their children's future and concentrated on establishing mosques and madrasas and creating a faith community. Riaz was amongst the very few migrants who were practising Muslims, praying five times a day and he went to Makkah in Saudi Arabia from the UK and performed the Hajj (pilgrimage). He became a community leader to whom the people would look for guidance and he would hire the town hall or a working men's club hall for the Muslims to pray in at religious Eid festivals. He also did voluntary community work and helped to set up the Indian Muslim Welfare Society along with other heads of the community and his friends. By now it was an appropriate time for the Muslim communities to establish a Muslim faith group.

Ahmed and other fellow students left school in 1966 and since they did not have any formal educational qualifications or skills, apart from knowing how to read and write, they had to follow the example of their fathers and work in the textile factories. This was not hard for them because they were given labouring work and as they were under the age of eighteen, they were paid half the wages earned by their parents. They were quite happy because the supervisors and white workers did not treat them as they did the other workers, because the youngsters were able to speak English and would not tolerate any nonsense so they knew that they could not oppress them. The supervisors were also able to talk to these youths in a Yorkshire accent, and the young Asians helped the employers and the Asian employees to communicate by acting as interpreters. The youths formed a group of friends and enjoyed working in factories and enjoyed the money they were earning.

Bashir and older members of the community spent most of their time working and enjoying their newly found happiness with good living standards and at the same time striving to preserve their identities and cultures. Their children on the other hand were growing up being educated and they started to communicate in English and learn about the British way of life. They began to feel less isolated and were regarded less as oddities.

Ahmed and his friends formed a network of about five

peers and enjoyed going to the local cafe, enjoyed eating sandwiches (without meat as they were not halal). They would listen to pop music on juke boxes and afterwards they would go to see a movie. Their favourite movies would be westerns, or maybe James Bond movies. If the movie was restricted to adults over sixteen due to its violent content and most of them were old enough to go but there was one who was sixteen years old, Ahmed and other friends drew a fine dotted moustache with a black marker on his upper lip and told him to stand on his tiptoes behind them at the ticket kiosk. The elderly lady who issued the tickets did suspect but took pity on these happy and excited youngsters and issued the ticket anyway and they watched the movie.

Jameela was now ten years old, enjoying school and sharing the newly- found culture at home with the family and making friends with some girls. They would visit each other frequently and Amina also created a network of female friends by meeting them when she took Jameela to school. So, the whole family was so busy with life that time was passing fast, the parents and children became healthy and put on weight compared to when they were back in India.

Asians up and down the UK now felt that they would

remain here indefinitely. Very few Pakistanis planned to bring their families over as the majority of them did not contemplate living here permanently. However, they too started feeling more at home here when BBC television started broadcasting special programmes for the Asian community in 1965. The first BBC broadcast was called Apna Hi Ghar Samajhiye, translated as "Make Yourself at Home," and was especially for the UK's newest inhabitants from South Asia. There was both a radio version, transmitted on the Home Service at 8.10 am before normal programming began, and a television edition on BBC 1 every Sunday at 9 am.

The language they adopted for the series was a mixture of simple Hindi and simple Urdu, as it aimed to help the Asian community to be part of Britain. By the beginning of the 1970s, the BBC had made significant changes and introduced a new programme "Nai Zindagi, Naya Jeevan" (New Life) because after about ten years the Asians were still coming to the UK. They needed to know the new sets of rules by which they would be expected to live in the UK and the BBC hoped that such an approach would help the Asians to assimilate more effectively. Since these programmes had

From Injustice to Self-Reliance

started, Asians would get up early in the morning and after having an Asian breakfast, the family would watch the programmes. They did feel connected with the content to some extent, but they were more interested in waiting for the end of the programme when for a few minutes they could enjoy the Asian music, sung by well-known local singers or by visiting singers from India and Pakistan.

However, whilst the BBC talked about integration or assimilation, the Asians were more concerned about preserving their culture. By now the Asian population in Dewsbury, Batley and the surrounding areas was increasing and reached a few thousand and was still growing as youngsters started arriving to marry and settle in the UK. As the community grew, so did the desire for cultural and religious activities. Many Asian workers started settling in Savile Town and so a separate organisation was formed, like that in Batley. They bought two terrace houses and made them into a mosque and madrassa under one roof, where prayers were performed five times a day and children received an Islamic education.

In Batley, Riaz helped to set up the Indian Muslim Welfare Society and bought a textile warehouse and converted it into a mosque and madrassa and so the residents began to establish a faith community. The new religious and educational institutions meant that they needed Islamic scholars to lead the prayers and teach in the madrassa and they were recruited from India. The scholars realised the benefits of living in the UK and admired the British Government for allowing them and the migrants to settle here, but they felt something was lacking even though the migrants were living comfortably with good lifestyles and so they started holding religious congregations here. These attracted hundreds of Muslims to attend from here and around Yorkshire and Lancashire which would last for a few days during the national holidays from work. Since the small mosque was not adequate to accommodate the congregation, they asked the employer at the factory almost next to the mosque, where many local Muslims worked, if they could give them some space and they were allowed to use empty halls free of charge, where people could listen to speeches and pray and sleep at nights. It was all managed by volunteers from the local community and food was also provided. The scholars acknowledged this kind gesture by the factory owner and talked about how friendly and tolerant

From Injustice to Self-Reliance

this country was. They told the Muslims to become respectable citizens and learn from their good behaviour, which is a fundamental part of Islam, but at the same time they talked about how the Muslims were not practising Islam by praying properly.

They did not frown upon the Muslims who were wearing suits but did say that such a way of dressing was improper for praying and the scholars set an example by wearing Islamic clothes to create the balance between adopting materialistic and spiritual lifestyles. The scholars also told the Muslims at the Mosque to start attending mosques more frequently and start taking some time out at weekends and during holidays for religious retreats at the local Mosque and to go around other mosques in the UK to learn more about Islam and from there visit other Muslims houses to invite them to their local Mosque to share Islamic knowledge. With such religious devotions in the UK, such activities inspired Muslims to adopt religious lifestyles, and this further led to more close-knit communities and gave them a greater facility. It was also time to have future visions for being in the UK. As the children started growing up, the parents had already started planning their marriages within the families back at home. There was no question about whether the children were ready to marry or not. Their parents felt that the family traditions had to continue, as they had already promised the extended family members. Even if the children did not entertain such ideas, they had no choice because boys and girls mixing and socialising outside the family was traditionally frowned upon and so it was not possible for them to choose their partners in majority of cases. However, the children at the same time valued the moral and financial support given by the family and as a result were able to sustain marriages.

The marriages were conducted by proxy with letters exchanged by post where the bride or bridegroom would go through the Islamic ceremony in India or Pakistan and the family would then send the agreement papers to the families here who would arrange for wedding ceremonies in the UK and send their agreement papers back to the bridegroom or bride's parents and the first time the couple would meet would be at Heathrow Airport. However, just like in India the marriages were sustained with moral and financial support from the family, and those children who came to the UK at an early age fitted in well with the traditional village lifestyle that the community had established. Therefore, there were no divorces even for the small numbers who were not happy with the forced or arranged marriages. It was a case of the family institutions, traditions, cultures, and prosperous lifestyles, with full citizenship and employment at the heart of the migrants. They always remembered and compared their life back at home where they were faced with the uncertainty of an agricultural lifestyle, simply because the villagers lived by cultivating a very limited domestic farm's products and had a fear of droughts, which meant that there was no guarantee that they could feed the family for the whole year. In comparison, Britain offered lifetime security.

From the Splendid Sun to the Glorious Pound

CHAPTER SEVEN

Living Another Life

The lives of the second generation of Asians were taking shape and their parents started getting them married. In 1970, Bashir and Amina also followed the general trend and arranged the marriage of their son to Farida who was two years younger than Ahmed and although he did not want to get married so soon, he had no choice in the matter and the marriage was organised. It was organised by proxy where the marriage was conducted Islamically in India, where Farida went through the simple ceremony at home without Ahmed and in the presence of her parents, extended family members and the Maulana (A religious scholar) and two witnesses who asked Farida if she would accept the proposal to marry Ahmed. She did not have any choice either and agreed because she was brought up to accept such traditions. Afterwards their parents sent a letter to Bashir with the evidence of the religious ceremony having taken place. After receiving the letter from India, Bashir organised a marriage ceremony which took place at the local mosque, where the letter of acceptance from Farida was presented to the mosque committee and the Maulana performed the Nikah (religious marriage ceremony).

The Islamic marriage certificate was issued and later in the afternoon a reception was held in a small hall where family and friends were treated with food including sweets. Within six months, Farida had arrived at Heathrow Airport. Ahmed accompanied by Bashir, Amina, Jameela, and the bride's auntie also arrived at the airport - by car, for which Bashir had hired a driver. At the airport the plane from India had landed and as the passengers started walking from the plane, Farida was spotted by the auntie who had only been living in the UK for about ten months and recognised her whilst Ahmed was nervously looking on and the auntie pointed out Farida to Ahmed and told him that was his wife, and soon they all met her at the arrivals gate. Ahmed and Farida looked at each other and Farida handed a box to Ahmed which contained records of Indian movie songs, which were the tradition in those days, to show that the couple had something in common. Afterwards, they all got in the car and Farida mostly talked to her auntie and about halfway they stopped at a motorway service station for a break and refuelling. They sat in the grass area to eat food

Living Another Life

which the auntie and Amina had brought with them. Ahmed did not talk much, and Farida was tired from the journey. She had never experienced city life like that in Bombay. Shopping and sightseeing there had made her tired, so she did not eat much and soon they were back on the motorway, and she fell asleep.

After reaching home they all had some food prepared by the next-door neighbour and afterwards, auntie and the neighbours went home, and the couple started married life with the task of getting to know each other. Farida had lived a secluded life in the village, which meant that she was not in a position to compare life in Indian cities with life in the UK, which in some ways made it easier for her to cope with her new life, particularly when everything had been arranged for her to settle down with the family. So, for her, it was easier than it had been for Amina when she first came to the UK. The only problem she was facing was missing her family and friends back at home and at such a young age it was difficult to forget that easily. In the meantime, the couple remained a bit nervous and felt like strangers. It took a few weeks to get to know each other but, with moral support from the family, sharing the domestic bills, and not being isolated socially meant that the couple were able to sustain married life and as the saying goes: 'love starts after marriage in the Asian community'. Such was the tradition for marriages as well as the tradition of living with parents which extended back thousands of years, and so for the parents, it was quite the norm, and they did not feel any guilt.

So far, the lifestyle for Asians had remained unchanged, apart from working in factories, buying better houses with inside toilets and bathroom facilities. Even though racial discrimination continued at work in some textile factories, the introduction of the Race Relations Board in 1966 following the passing of the Race Relations Act in 1965 gave the migrants confidence to further their dreams and ambitions in the UK. The Act outlawed discrimination on the grounds of colour, race, or ethnic or national origin in public places in Great Britain. The remit of the Board was to consider complaints under the Act. It dealt with 327 complaints of racial discrimination in 1966. This gave all the migrant communities in the UK confidence in the successive British governments, and they felt that they would be able to live a dignified life.

However, what they never envisaged was that something

Living Another Life

was lurking in the background and waiting to be explored. One day, Asians around the UK woke up to a news headline that sent a shockwave through their community. "The Rivers of Blood" speech was made by MP Enoch Powell on 20 April 1968 at a meeting of the Conservative Political Centre in Birmingham, UK. His speech strongly criticised mass immigration, especially commonwealth migrants, to the UK as well as the proposed Race Relations Bill.

The Conservative leader, Edward Heath, sacked Powell from his post as Shadow Defence Secretary. Heath went on a BBC television current affairs programme and said 'I dismissed Mr Powell because I believed his speech was inflammatory and liable to damage race relations. I am determined to do everything I can to prevent racial problems from developing into civil strife I don't believe the great majority of the British people share Mr Powell's way of putting his views in his speech' What shocked the Asians most was that Enoch Powell wanted legislation to repatriate 200,000 Asian migrants a year, giving £1,000 to each individual Asian migrant. Since the vast majority of Asians were farmers or small businessmen and did not know much about politics, they did not understand the political system in the UK and wondered whether one day they would have to leave the UK, and this filled them with fear of an uncertain future. However, with opposition from most politicians and reassurances from the government, the Asians began to feel that they would not be repatriated and so the shock was short-lived and their trust in the successive British governments was in some ways reinstated, and they could get on with their lives.

Ahmed and Farida stayed with his parents and whilst he worked in the factory, she remained a housewife and shared the domestic tasks with Amina. Ahmed and Farida would go shopping at the weekend and visit friends and people from neighbouring villages who had settled here. The women were not allowed to go out to cinemas so Ahmed would meet up with his friends at the weekend and venture out to other cities like Leeds and Bradford and go to a café and then watch movies in the evening. Almost all of Ahmed's school friends who studied with him in the special class at school went to work in the textile factories, got married to girls in India and shared the same youth culture, which did not present any problems with their wives because they were brought up to be housewives and mostly stayed at home. As the youngsters learnt more about British culture, spoke English, and shared a different sense of humour compared to that of the traditional Asian community, they started going out to discos in town and a small minority of them even started drinking alcohol. They made sure the parents did not find out and this kind of cheeky behaviour made them feel adventurous.

The vast majority of Asians bought their own houses. Renting had never appealed to them, as it was a tradition from back home to have their own homes, and their quality of life improved tremendously. However, after "The Rivers of Blood" speech the Asian migrants became the victims of racial attacks and Enoch Powell was blamed for the violent attacks against British Asians called Paki-bashing, which became frequent after the speech. These attacks peaked later in 1968 and the Asian community throughout suffered abuse and physical attacks whether they were going to work or shopping. Abuse such as 'go back where you have come from you Pakis' was common, but what the Asians valued most was the good and sensible behaviour of the majority of white people and that gave them reassurance that, although they were going through a difficult time, there was the hope of better days ahead of them.

At the same time, some young Asians got fed up with working in factories without any career prospects and they left these jobs and attended college to study advanced courses, for which they were given grants from the Employment department, so they could have better career prospects. The classes consisted of adults from different backgrounds and ages, including some who did not speak much English and so the lessons were organised to suit individual needs. They enjoyed the environment of being at a college where there were Jamaicans, Indians, Pakistanis, and Eastern Europeans with different racial and cultural backgrounds. An equally mixed sense of humour led to lots of banter when they were learning, turning their English language mistakes into comedy. They were taught English, maths, British history, and had elocution lessons and, after a year, the younger students were better placed to find employment, having the ability to communicate in English without much difficulty. The Employment department who financed the course found them employment for more skilled jobs and a few even went on to further education. The older students went back to the textile factories or used the education they had received to start small businesses like opening market stalls and driving taxis.

The Asians started moving forward with the aim of improving their quality of life still further and for those who were educated back home, it was natural for them to start their own businesses. Riaz, Bashir's cousin, sold his corner shop and bought a large warehouse in Bradford in partnership with a Pakistani friend and started a new wholesale business importing spices, rice, lentils and almost all the necessary goods for cooking Asian food. They imported goods from the Indian subcontinent and Africa and supplied them to retailers. It was a huge investment of their own money as well as loans from the bank. The business was doing well and, as the textile industry was starting to decline, many Asians started opening corner shops and there was a better future ahead for them all. Most of the businesses were run by family members and they also employed newly arrived Asian youths who got married to girls in the UK.

Since they did not speak much English, working for other Asians suited them well. Apart from those who set up in business for themselves, the majority of Asians continued working in textile mills and their weekend entertainment consisted of wrestling, going to movies and socialising with family and friends. Those who were educated in India formed a group called "Gujarati Poetry Writers Circle", which meant the weekend amusements expanded to include the recitation of poems at home as well as at public halls. They invited various members of the community so that they could be entertained and have the opportunity to socialise over the free meals provided there.

Their poetry spoke of religion, culture, romance, and their experiences of living in the UK and India. They wrote about how some of them had to lower their status and had to work in factories. By now the Pakistani community was following the example of the Indian community and was starting to bring over their families to enjoy the good lifestyle. Like the Indians, they adopted the traditional culture of arranged marriages from back home and those educated in Pakistan in the Urdu language formed their own cultural activities of poetry and folk songs, which the Indians also enjoyed because they were able to understand Urdu and Hindi which are similar and so it was easy for them to be entertained.

Whilst the feel-good factors continued, Asians were faced with another shock when they saw the headlines in the British media, concerning a woman who arrived at Heathrow on 24 January 1979 seeking entry as the fiancée of a man living in Southall. She consented to undergo a gynaecological examination 'which may be vaginal if necessary' on the instructions of an immigration officer. The woman, a 35-year-old teacher, was examined by a male doctor. The Home Office claimed that such tests helped them to identify women who attempted to enter the country illegally, by establishing whether a woman was a bona fide fiancée. A test of this nature assumed that, if a Hindu woman was found to be a virgin, she would be believed to be unmarried and if she was found not to be one, she would not be believed. A Home Office spokesman stated that such an examination was 'not standard practice for all immigrant women' - it was dependent on the immigration officer and whether he was satisfied that the passenger was all she claimed to be.

The disclosure of this incident created controversy. In the House of Commons, Prime Minister James Callaghan said that every MP would be 'disturbed' by the matter and Ms Jo Richardson, Labour MP for Barking tabled a series of

From the Splendid Sun to the Glorious Pound

Parliamentary Questions to determine how long the practice of virginity testing of immigrants had been going on. Mr Nacarats, the Deputy Indian High Commissioner met Mr Evan Luard, an undersecretary of state for the Foreign Office to register a formal protest. Although the woman was Hindu, the Muslim Asians also felt that this was insulting to the people from the Indian subcontinent. However, the Racial Equality and Equal Opportunities Commission issued a joint statement condemning the practice and so the Asians felt a sense of comfort and their desire to settle here permanently continued unchanged.

Asians had settled in their thousands across West Yorkshire and when the headmaster from the local school in Batley went for a holiday in India, he was advised by the local Indians in Batley that he should visit their villages back home. When he and his wife did this, they were given a warm welcome, particularly by the relatives of the families in the UK as the villagers all came to meet them. They were greeted with garlands and treated to traditional home-cooked village-style food made with home-grown organic vegetables and goat meat, as well as a village tour. Whilst the couple were doing a walkabout in a village where one of the families

Living Another Life

in Batley had suggested they visit, they saw a street where, on one side, the rows of houses were occupied whilst on the opposite side, the rows of houses were empty, so the headmaster asked what had happened to the inhabitants and the villagers told him that they were living in Batley. When the headmaster came back to Batley, he asked the people who came from that village why they were still living in the UK when their villages were so wonderful, and the people were always smiling despite the poverty and living a simple life. The headmaster said that what with the guaranteed sunshine, beautiful warm weather, the open spaces with fresh air, hospitable people, and home-grown organic food, he and his wife found it difficult to understand why they stayed in the UK. The Indians replied that they had left for the sake of the future generations, the financial security, free education, healthcare, and the friendliness of the British people. The granting of British citizenship made them happy and comfortable.

Here, many immigrants were turning to their faith and, as more migrants started coming and the population grew, so the need for more madrasas also grew. Classes for children from age six to twelve were being taught in the cellars of houses with the same curriculum as back home. Maulana from India were recruited to teach the children from five to seven in the evenings daily from Monday to Friday. The parents would pay fees which were not much but enough to pay the teacher's wages. The children at the madrasa were taught an Islamic education and good behaviour by the teacher who was always equipped with a bamboo stick. To the dismay of the parents, if a child misbehaved or made mistakes whilst reciting, they were beaten with this stick on their hand. After a few years, a small number of parents complained about it to the police. This led to a reminder of the illegality of hitting children and a threat of legal action if there were future occurrences. The practice ceased.

Whilst the Muslim communities in Dewsbury and Batley and throughout the UK were trying to preserve their identity and culture, they did not want anything to do with the cultural changes which were happening outside their communities in the UK and throughout the western countries. The Muslims were oblivious to such changes and the only knowledge they had of them was by seeing the news coverage of the riots, protests, and movements and they were not directly affected. In the mid-1960s youth around the world became increasingly aware of social issues, such as war and starvation, and found many causes such as anti-poverty, and anti-war, to support. Many students protested loudly against the Vietnam War, which continued until 1975. The youth found their own culture of hippies, drugs, and pop music. These changes were partly defiant counterculture: men and women alike would wear garments with garish, abstract patterns in bold colours that emphasised their youth, their freedom and their independence from their parents and traditional society.

In India, gurus would influence the Western youth, and celebrities such as pop groups and Hollywood actors started following the gurus and so many went to India to participate in the newly-discovered cultural revolution. They turned to drugs, and most hippies believed that drugs such as LSD and marijuana were valuable tools for spiritual growth. As a result, many hippies often incorporated drugs into their spiritual practices such as meditation or yoga. They did this even though most Indian gurus believed that such drugs blocked spiritual development and discouraged their use. Although some hippies avoided drugs, it is fair to say that the broader hippie culture nevertheless continued to view drugs as a valid form of personal fulfilment, and often associated them with non-traditional modes of spirituality. The Indian culture had a tremendous influence on the broader hippie culture. As a result, practices such as burning incense, displaying Indian art, listening to Indian music, using mala (prayer) beads, as well as wearing colourful Indian-style clothing, becoming vegetarian, performing meditation, and practising yoga became popular even among hippies who did not pursue the deeper philosophies. Although this began slowly, these trends grew in acceptance.

The Muslims were never interested in such changes as they perceived it as a negative culture leading toward disaster. Indian Muslims who grew up in India knew too well that none of their ancestors followed such a culture. They believed that they would not benefit from such a culture which went against their faith, and instead believed that survival lay in their own culture and religious beliefs which they were more eager to continue enforcing. Their aim was to protect future generations against immorality but without challenging other non-Muslim communities, so they adopted the notions that they must better themselves, be good to others and live a dignified life. In the meantime, successive

British governments recognised and encouraged the right of the migrants to practise their faiths and cultures by facilitating the building of self-financed places of worship. As the years passed, the Muslims had to learn to tolerate the cultural differences that their youngsters were adopting, such as fashion and going to cinemas and concerts, but lines were drawn when it came to drugs and other negative activities that would have a detrimental effect on their lifestyle. As a result, the Dewsbury and Batley Muslim faith leaders established Tablighi Jamaat's missionary activity in the UK and throughout Europe and more mosques were being built.

Ahmed was representative of this younger generation. He was becoming more fashion-conscious and started going out to movies and eating out. He had learned to drive and bought a small second-hand van. At the weekends, he would go to Bradford and would take his friends for a meal at an Indian restaurant, in return his friends would pay him money for taking them there. The youngsters grew their hair long, wore bell-bottom trousers, jeans, and cheesecloth shirts, like the white youngsters. Some of them listened to English pop music, Indian movie songs and even imitated their favourite singers such as David Bowie, the Rolling Stones, Elvis

From the Splendid Sun to the Glorious Pound

Presley as they adopted both English and Asian cultures. Whereas their female counterparts were not allowed to go out to see movies Instead, they went shopping with friends and adopted contemporary Indian fashion like the Indian movie actresses. Usman, one of Ahmed's friends was even more westernised and forward-looking and, since they were both interested in cars, they decided to build a beach buggy, which was an immensely popular trend amongst the white youths.

They bought an old car and removed the roof, bought trendy steering, a dashboard, and seats bought from a scrapyard to suit the buggy. They assembled it themselves and took it to a friend who spray painted it for them in multiple colours and patterns with 'Passion Wagon' written on the side. This was a great achievement for them both, particularly for Ahmed who had not been able to speak English when he first came to the UK, and he felt that he was moving on and enjoying British life. They would venture out in the beach buggy with other friends throughout Yorkshire to parks and the seaside. They enjoyed driving in open countryside, wearing sunglasses, and listening to music.

By 1972, the Asians were generally feeling that they were

a part of Britain when they saw yet another shocking story on the television news. Around 60,000 Ugandan Asians were given 90 days to leave Uganda by President Idi Amin, and those Ugandan refugees who were UK passport holders, fleeing the persecution of the country's military dictatorship, had arrived in Britain. They were to be re-housed in the UK by the Ugandan Resettlement Board established by the British government. The refugees were speedily evacuated in their thousands by the British government. President Amin had denounced the Ugandan Asians as "bloodsuckers" and warned that any remaining in the country after 8 November risked being imprisoned in military camps. The Asians in Uganda were mainly farmers or owned businesses and had made excellent progress over the years with high living standards. They had to abandon everything and arrived here penniless. When the Indians already settled in the UK saw these images on British TV, they were again in shock, and it also reminded the older Indians of the time when the first military rule began in Burma in 1958 and the direct military rule started when the army took power through a coup d'état when the Indian migrants became refugees. Thousands had to abandon their prosperous lifestyles and, penniless, had to walk about 2000 miles to India. So, the Indian migrants in the UK could not help thinking and asking themselves about their future in the UK. Could it happen here? But this just remained a thought as they realised that Britain was not a third world country and the support, they had received so far was enough to have trust in the democracy and so they continued moving forward.

As the saying goes in the UK "an Englishman's house is his castle," so for the Asians, this type of culture suited them well. In addition, more Asians were becoming debt-free and were able to save money the traditional way. Lending money to each other continued and those who wanted to buy bigger and better houses also started applying for mortgages. Therefore, although the Asians' lives had been something of a roller coaster up to the present time, they were appreciative of what this country had given them, and they were quite content with it. In return, the traditional Asians would say that they should pray for the Indigenous community and successive governments for allowing them to have a new life. Otherwise, what would have happened to them, back home with an increasing level of poverty? Even if they had a little in the way of savings, a drought or family illness could wipe out entire savings due to the healthcare cost. Here in the UK, they were achieving prosperity at a faster rate compared with back at home. Here, health costs would be covered by the National Health Service, even for expensive operations. Free education was provided and the vast variety of food on offer at supermarkets was affordable. All of this meant that they lived with relative ease and were able to plan such things as marrying their children without having to worry about the expense as they were able to save enough money. The freedom to practise their religion and culture without any pre-conditions was the most important benefit for them, as it helped towards fulfilling their dreams and ambitions of making Britain their home.

From the Splendid Sun to the Glorious Pound

CHAPTER EIGHT

Living With Mixed Blessings

Since 1972 the Asians had been moving away from a poverty-stricken life. Many owned cars, particularly the youngsters who were more outgoing and were creating their own youth culture, wanting to spend more money and enjoy being part of Britain. By now, Asian families had started sharing in some elements of British culture. For example, they got to know more about the Royal Family and at Christmas, they too started listening to The Queen's Christmas speech on Christmas day. This is something of a British institution and the Asians appreciated the Queen sending greetings to the Commonwealth countries.

Also, the Asian youths in the UK were getting married in their hundreds and thus the population was increasing with the births of their children and being Muslim meant they did not use contraception. Jameela had left school aged 16 with six GCSEs. She could have gone on to further education but, due to the family being traditionalists and not able to realise or not being sure of the future of Asian women in the UK, combined with the culture of keeping it in the family meant that she was to marry a cousin, Amina's sister's son Musa. At 19-years-old, he was a year younger than Jameela. He lived in India and was educated in Gujarati and Hindi but not to the level of Jameela. Bashir and Amina assumed that this was the best decision for the whole of the extended family and within a year, Jameela's marriage was arranged. This time the couple had an opportunity to exchange photographs of each other six months before Musa arrived in the UK. Musa arrived at Heathrow Airport and Bashir, Farida Amina, and Jameela went to receive him. He was smartly dressed like an Indian actor, with long hair, moustache, long sideburns, and bell-bottom trousers. Jameela, brought up in the UK, was not shy and they looked at each other and headed towards the motorway in the family car which Ahmed was driving. Musa despite his tiredness interacted well with the family and talked about the family back home. He had been able to go to the cities in India because his family was a bit better off and, with the financial support from Amina and Bashir, were doing well in their farming business.

Jameela was talkative which Musa found a bit surprising because he had expected her to be shy and quieter like the girls in his village, but then having a ride in the family-owned car and a brighter future waiting for him in the UK, he was happy to show respect to the family. They stopped for a break at a service station to refuel They started eating and got some chicken masala from a bag along with samosas and chapatis, Musa liked the chicken which was somewhat different from the chicken in India. Here, the chicken was bigger with lots of meat on it which Musa had already heard about back at home. In fact, when Indians went back to India to visit, they normally took cooked spicy chicken for the relatives, who would come from the village to pick them up. Outside the airport, they would get treated to chicken and, by then, the masalas had blended well and became even tastier. Musa was informed that he was to stay with a member of the extended family as, according to Islamic tradition, the engaged couple were not allowed to stay under the same roof, until they got married, although they were allowed to see each other, in the presence of the family members only. Within two months the couple got married at the local Mosque and the wedding reception was held at a school hall, with about five hundred guests.

There were different kinds of celebrations compared with Ahmed's wedding. Now, more young people were

From the Splendid Sun to the Glorious Pound

enjoying Indian songs, wore fashionable clothes and there were plentiful tasty foods. Musa remained a bit shy on the stage, but Jameela was certainly not shy and interacted with jokes and laughing with the guests, particularly with her school friends, but poor Musa felt a bit alienated. Afterwards, the family gave away the bride to Musa and the extended family with whom he was staying, Ahmed's family. Jameela's friends got emotional and cried to a sad Indian song with the words 'take blessings from the parents and may you have a happy future with your new life and with your husband' Jameela hugged family members and friends and cried as such was the tradition from back home.

However, the couple stayed with Jameela's family and, although the house was not big enough for all of them, the newly married couple managed for two years, so it gave them time to settle into their marriage. Musa got a job in a factory and since the family took care of them Musa and Jameela were able to save some money. Bashir and Amina helped them financially to buy a house. Musa borrowed the rest of the money from relatives and friends, and they moved to their own small house. Musa who could not speak English relied on Jameela to organise the running of the house such as paying the domestic bills and shopping. All he had to do was to work and bring in wages. Their different upbringings did present some minor problems with the marriage at first, such as misunderstanding senses of humour which were different to people in India and Musa being a village boy and Jameela's personality being more expressive. Still, she managed to live with it, the family sorted any problems between them and so like many other similar marriages in the Asian community they have learned to sustain married life. Also, within the close-knit Muslim community here, the divorce rates were non-existent and there was hardly any mental illness. All was down to the family and community support and not being socially isolated - and it all worked very well.

A few younger workers who were educated in India and Pakistan and were able to communicate in English fairly well were looking to find work where they would have better status and could take control of their hours of work. So, they started leaving the factory work and started driving taxis and buses. By now the Asians were earning a good living and earning more than in the factories. They started buying cars which allowed them to work as driving instructors.

From the Splendid Sun to the Glorious Pound

Furthermore, it gave them better status and they were able to work flexible hours and so spend more time with their families. As the Muslims started earning more because their children were earning wages, they were able to save money and the parents started going for Hajj (Islamic pilgrimage) to Makkah in Saudi Arabia and many went back home to visit families and, after a couple of years, they sometimes invited their parents to the UK. Many Pakistanis were slowly settling here with their families. There were still some who decided to visit home more frequently and kept their families in Pakistan because they had not thought of staying in the UK permanently. However, overall, Asians were becoming part of Britain and their brave efforts of going through the challenges of settling in the UK further exemplified their commitment to fulfilling their dreams. With a prosperous future in mind, they were moving forward, and they continued with the setting up of the closely-knit community and with their commitment to support each other. Some of the younger members of the community played cricket at weekends and established their leagues and would go around Yorkshire and Lancashire to organise matches. Those who were brought to the UK took interest in British football and

Living With Mixed Blessings

started playing football amongst themselves and set up Asian Football leagues around the country and organised football matches in Yorkshire and Lancashire.

Britain had been known as the workshop of the world but now the textile industry started declining in Yorkshire and Lancashire, which meant that many workers were becoming the victims of redundancy and thus had to register with the Employment Department, but since they had no other skills, it was difficult to find alternative employment. It was not in their interest to remain unemployed for any length of time, so many opted for self-employment because they had some business experience as farmers back at home. They were able to sell some goods like car parts or clothes, to open small furniture or carpet shops. A few young Asians learned trades at government training centres to work as motor mechanics, painters, decorators. They opened wholesale meat supplier businesses, bed manufacturing, and selling second-hand cars from home. By 1976, there were three million unemployed in the UK and many of them were Asian and black immigrants, which led to further discrimination as many right-wingers were using Asians and black people as scapegoats for the unemployment statistics and accused them of not integrating into British society. The extreme right-wing organisations started attacking Asians physically in the streets again, or at work in their taxis or on Asian market stalls and desecrating Muslim cemeteries.

However, the British government further repealed the Race Relations Act in 1968 and established local Community Relations Councils for eradicating racial discrimination and liaised with the local authorities and the police to give the migrants protection from racial discrimination. The local Community Relations Council in Dewsbury played an important part in building good relations between the whites and Asians by organising summer playgroups consisting of children from both communities and the volunteers mostly students were also recruited from both the white and Asians locally, around the country and from European countries. The playgroup leaders took the Asian and white kids on trips to parks, museums, the seaside and played sports with them.

In the meantime, the Asian students at the college in Dewsbury set up an organisation called "Asian Students Associations" because they felt left out socially and their main function was to convince the Student Union committee consisting of all whites to finance social evenings at the

Living With Mixed Blessings

Town Hall and invite the community to enjoy an Asian variety show with performers in different cultural aspects such as Asian music, Asian dance, drama and selling Asian food, They also organised sports with the white students and such initiatives were welcomed by the Principal who attended the shows. The members of the Asian community also attended the various shows and felt proud of their young people educating themselves and also organising Asian cultural activities.

Whilst the Asians remained positive as the Government was trying to make them feel at home, all seemed fine in Dewsbury and Batley until an Asian student at the Dewsbury and Batley College of Further Education was given a leaflet by a fellow, white, student who happened to be a member of an extreme right-wing political party who were to march in Dewsbury demanding the repatriation of the Asians. The Asian Students Association immediately called a meeting and showed their disgust when they approached the white student who had distributed the leaflet. He defended it and claimed that his party was not a racist organisation.

However, one of the Asian students knew a white person who was a member of staff at an Advice Centre in Batley

From the Splendid Sun to the Glorious Pound

who was helping unemployed people from different backgrounds who were victims of poverty. The white person was invited to meet with the Asian students who wanted to hold a counter-demonstration against the extreme right-wing party and he brought a Socialists Workers newspaper and said that he would be happy to bring his socialist members from around Yorkshire to participate in a counter, anti-fascist and racist demonstration against the Extreme Right Wing Political Party. The next day the representatives from the Asian students' associations and the white Socialists went around the Asian and white communities to distribute leaflets telling them to join the counter-demonstration. Within a week about a hundred Extreme Right Wing Party members held a march in Dewsbury Town chanting 'send them back home', and about three hundred held a counter-demonstration chanting 'Here to stay', The police had the task of making sure that the groups did not clash and, although some tried to get through the police lines to reach the Extreme Right Wing Party march, they were prevented by the police, a few were arrested and later fined.

Ahmed and his wife remained with their parents and bought a bigger house because Jameela gave birth to a baby girl and generally life had improved a lot for the Asians. They did not have to bring live chickens home because by now some Halal butcher shops had opened and one of the Indian businessmen who had started in a corner shop in Dewsbury bought a small supermarket in the heart of the Asian community in Batley which was run by family members. They also allowed the community to pay for their shopping within a month and the shoppers were enjoying this concession. Asians have always been fond of fresh fish which they used to catch back home from the local rivers. Here, the fish bought from the fishmongers in the market did not taste the same. So, the owner of the new mini-supermarket had an idea: he decided to go to Grimsby, a seaside town in Yorkshire, every Monday where he would purchase freshly caught fish and collect it at around 4 am, so by the time his shop opened, shoppers would be queuing to buy whole pieces of fresh fish and this was a delicacy on their dinner tables every Monday. It also gave the women a chance to meet up and socialise as they were gathering outside the shop or on their way home. Also, there were fresh Indian vegetables from back home imported by wholesalers, but by the time they were consumed they would be at least four days old so the taste was not the same as back home but then for the Asians, this was better than life in India and Pakistan and they did not have to worry about how much they were able to consume as they could afford to pay.

At last, they had started feeling more at home by now and because they were Muslims, their faith beliefs were always very strong despite the racists using them as scapegoats for the economic problems Britain was facing. They remained strong and had a belief that being happy and sad is part of life but not as harsh as back home and, God willing, they would succeed with their brighter future in Britain. Furthermore, they felt that the respect and support given by the British government and the majority of indigenous people were more than they had expected. They were also enjoying the religious festivals such as Eid in a big way. The men were able to go to the Mosques in their area and meet friends and families and the women would cook a variety of delicious Eid dishes and later in the afternoon, they visited extended families or friends where they would have evening meals. Everyone in the community could have prosperous Eid festivities (unlike back at home where only the rich would eat expensive meals at Eid) and the poor ones who could not afford it at home were now part of one class and enjoying the same lifestyle.

From the Splendid Sun to the Glorious Pound

CHAPTER NINE

The Tripartite Community and the Generation Gap

From 1976 onwards migrants were faced yet again with new challenges: the textile industry was drastically declining, and many businesses had closed which started to impact their livelihoods. Even those who were lucky enough to be working were still facing racial discrimination in textile mills. However, young Asians were conscious of how prevalent racism still was in the UK and with the rising growth of extreme right-wing organisations, they felt the need to organise themselves. The students who had left Dewsbury college reunited and formed the Dewsbury and Batley Asian Youth Organisation (AYO) to campaign against racial discrimination and to help the community with their problems, such as communication problems with English language, social and welfare problems. Their main goals were to instil confidence and positivity amongst youths to move forward with their education, careers and learning skills.

From the Splendid Sun to the Glorious Pound

The Asian Youth Organisation consisted of Indians and Pakistanis and within six months they had about three hundred members from working-class to professionals, alongside science, business studies and social science students. On one occasion, a member, Rafiq approached the AYO chairman Salim and informed him that some Asian workers had been sacked from a textile factory because they had demanded a better hourly rate for overtime work and so went on strike, which was not the case with white workers. There were still a few textile factories remaining and, with the high unemployment rates, they were not so desperate to recruit workers. They could afford to treat the Asian workers differently. After hearing this, Salim advised the workers to go back to the factory and picket outside and he agreed to meet them there. So, the next day the workers went back to the factory, and the chairman of the Asian Youth Organisation and two of his committee members met the workers outside the factory. After listening to their story, the chairman asked to speak to the manager, who came and asked the youths who they were.

The chairman, dressed in a long, light brown tweed winter overcoat with a long, striped scarf and round, metal

The Tripartite Community and the Generation Gap

John Lennon style glasses, pretended to be a journalist and demanded an explanation as to why the Asian workers were treated differently. The manager was not able to handle this, as he had never come across a young Asian man who spoke better English than he did, so asked the chairman to wait whilst he called the company director. After about half an hour the director middle-aged, wearing a suit and tie - arrived in a Rolls Royce. He was immediately confronted by Salim who said frankly that the treatment of the workers was illegal according to the Government Race Relations Act and that he would expose it in a newspaper. The Asian workers were looking on and were pleasantly surprised and impressed by these three brave youths representing them and being so confident. The director had a brief discussion with the manager and then made a speech in front of the workers and said that the supervisor had made an error, and his staff would be made aware of the Race Relations Act. With heartfelt apologies, the director reinstated the workers and granted them their full hourly rates, much to the joy and elation of the workers. They warmly embraced the young men who had assisted them, expressing their gratitude for their help and support.

From the Splendid Sun to the Glorious Pound

The community took pride in the next generation's achievements, pleased with their acquisition of skills beyond textile work and even higher education. With their children's future in mind, the parents overlooked the youths' behaviour, welcoming the fusion of traditionalism and Western culture that came with their new way of life. However, this also marked the beginning of a generation gap divide between the old and the new, as the youths' upbringing and education in the UK had instilled in them a sense of self-assurance and confidence, which at times clashed with traditional values. However, the nuclear family did not disappear completely, and the family still needed to fulfil their emotional and economic needs and so it had no alternative other than to support each other as the supply and demands are met by the family and community and in return, they got awarded by favours. Furthermore, the Asian community was becoming aware that economic growth and individualism alone does not provide happiness so, even with the generation gap, the parents felt comfortable with how the community was evolving, which led to the tripartite community and the generation gap.

Therefore, what happened was that certain sections of

The Tripartite Community and the Generation Gap

the community adopted a more faith-related lifestyle, others worked and lived a family-oriented life such as going to the movies and socialising with friends and family, whilst the young Muslims were faced with a generations gap and were more inclined towards shaping their own future. Although they socialised with family and friends within the community, they also started socialising with white friends such as in sports and going for meals and a few also went to discotheques. By now the white youngsters were getting to know the Asian community and were being attracted to the taste of delicious Indian and Pakistani food.

The elders, despite not having much knowledge of the rapidly changing British society, tried their best to instil Asian culture into the youngsters brought up and educated here, but found it rather difficult. Having been told to 'mind their own business' parents tended to leave the youngsters to themselves, as long as they did not slip too far into the Western culture. They feared that their children would neither belong to the Muslim community nor the English community, which meant that they would feel alienated with an uncertain future. Bashir and his family were also fine with that and whilst Bashir and Amina were turning towards their religion, Ahmed was busy with his business venture and Jameela would help her mother with the business. Jameela followed her parents and remained focused on domesticity, because of the notion that a girl's duty should be to get married and have a family life.

The Muslims did not have any difficulties with maintaining their cultural and religious identity and their appreciation continued to grow for successive British governments that allowed them such freedom, but the racial discrimination against the Asians continued both in terms of institutional racism and physical attacks throughout the UK. The older generations did not want to act, fearing a racist backlash and did not want to be branded as troublemakers. They believed that if they were allowed the freedom to live in their close-knit communities with their culture and religion everything would be fine. Also, those who had participated in the struggle against British Colonial rule in India remembered how much people had sacrificed to gain independence and so they felt it was useless to campaign against racism on British home ground, but the second generation of Asians were taking a different approach.

From 1974 onwards the physical attacks by the minority

of white racists were increasing throughout the UK and the Asian youth being brought up here was not going to tolerate such intimidation from the extreme right-wing groups. So, up and down the country and through the Dewsbury and Batley Asian Youth Organisation they continued to campaign against racist attacks and demand equality in employment. They were able to organise hundreds of Asian counter-demonstrations against the extreme right wing who would come from around the country in small numbers, but incited racism and recruited local white people, mainly youths, from each area.

They were using Asians as scapegoats for the high unemployment figures which had risen to three million in the UK. The Asian youths on the other hand were supported by the trade unions, the Labour Party, and other left-wing socialist organisations. Similarly, there were Asian youths around the country from different backgrounds such as Muslims, Hindus and Sikhs who also organised themselves, as they too became the victims of racist attacks. The organisations were known as the Asian Youth Movements, and the Bradford Asian Youth Movement advised the Dewsbury and Batley Asian Youth Organisation to change its name to 'movement.' The organisers declined the offer and kept it as Asian Youth Organisation, but they jointly campaigned against racism. The Jewish community in the UK also started campaigning against the extreme right wing's antisemitic racist organisations, remembering how they suffered under Nazi Fascism, when millions of Jews were murdered. As a result, an anti-Nazi League was formed consisting of people from different backgrounds who were the victims of racism, and this effectively campaigned throughout the UK. Through the media, they lobbied successive governments to ban the racist organisations.

The Dewsbury and Batley Asian Youth Organisation also took their members to other towns and cities around Yorkshire, Lancashire, the Midlands and London, areas such as Southall with the largest population of Sikhs and Harringay. They attended anti-racism rallies and joined in Rock Against Racism concerts, where celebrities performed and speeches were made by many multi-ethnic leaders and left-wing politicians. The Asian youths attended many meetings and conferences organised by the left-wing white working-class who supported the campaign against racism. The Asian Youths and anti-Nazi League campaigned jointly

The Tripartite Community and the Generation Gap

and held counterdemonstrations locally, they adopted slogans such as 'Black and White must unite, here to stay, here to fight.' This allowed the young Asian men to go to many towns and cities up and down the country where they came across people from different cultural, racial, and political backgrounds. Having been brought up in close community settings, particularly the local Muslims from this area, it was an eye-opener, and they realised the importance of meeting and appreciating people with different cultural backgrounds.

The Bradford Asian Youth Movement was campaigning for Anwar Ditta who was married with two children in the UK to a British-born Pakistani wife but was about to be deported to Pakistan by the British Immigration Authority who were claiming that he entered illegally. The Dewsbury and Batley Asian Youth Organisation also supported such campaigns, and they made history by inviting Mrs Ditta to Dewsbury Town Hall to speak at a conference which was held to support her campaign. She was the first-ever female Asian to speak at Dewsbury Town Hall. She told the conference that she was determined to fight for justice and the fact that so many young people brought up in the UK

From the Splendid Sun to the Glorious Pound

were supporting her, gave her added confidence and she would not rest until justice was served. After a couple of years, Anwar Ditta's case was reported in a documentary on British television and the case was further highlighted in the wider media. A few months after, the Home Office looked carefully at Anwar Ditta's case and he was given full rights to stay in the UK permanently, thanks to the Bradford Asian Youth Movement, the left-wing British media and left-wing white organisations who helped to reunite the Anwar family.

The second-generation Asians, despite considering Britain their home, felt angry that their parents had been treated unfairly and now that the textile industry was declining drastically and many Asian workers were becoming unemployed, treated as though they were no longer needed, it prompted them to continue with their campaign against racism. In Dewsbury and Batley's Asian community, a few years later, some remained unemployed and retired, while others who were of working age became self-employed. Many chose to work as taxi drivers, while some ventured into manufacturing, such as beds and household furniture.

To succeed, they relied on financial support from their community and personal savings, working long and unsociable hours. As their businesses grew, they began hiring workers from both the Asian and White communities. Interestingly, the textile factories they had once worked in were now owned by Asians who had started manufacturing beds, contributing to their newfound affluence within a couple of years. As far as their faith was concerned, a couple more mosques were established by converting two or three terrace houses into a mosque in Dewsbury and in Batley, a former textile factory was converted into a mosque along with a church building which was also bought and converted to a mosque.

In 1982, the Markaz Masjid (Central Mosque) also known as the Dewsbury Markaz or Dar ul 'Ulum (House of Knowledge) which is in the Savile Town area of Dewsbury was built. It has a maximum capacity of 4,000, is one of the largest mosques in Europe, as well as being the European headquarters of the movement and housing the Institute of Education for boys aged 13-25. The mosque serves as a centre for Tablighi Jamaat's missionary activity throughout Europe, the founder of Dewsbury Markaz who remained its figurehead until he died in 2016. Muslims from around the UK would come and stay at the centre and then small groups of people would be sent to different towns and cities in the UK where they would stay at the local mosque. From there, they would go door to door and invite fellow Muslims to join them, learn Islamic knowledge and become practising Muslims.

As a result, many started wearing Islamic clothes, such as men's Muslim- style trousers which are comfortable for praying and they would wear shirts but not tucked into trousers. Thus, it would be much easier for them to pray on prayer mats, and many started growing beards following the principles of spiritually changing behaviours to serve God and the communities. As a result, there were growing numbers of Muslims who were becoming practising Muslims and living life according to the teaching of the Prophet Mohammed, with good behaviour and living as respectable citizens. Ahmed also started attending the Markaz with his father and became a practising Muslim and made some friends. Later, one of these friends became his business partner and with further investment, the bed manufacturing business grew and moved to a bigger factory.

The Community Relations Council in Dewsbury employed a Hindu Community Relations Officer, Narendra

The Tripartite Community and the Generation Gap

Sharma, because of his education in community and race relations. He already had experience working with the community in Bradford, he spoke Hindi and was able to communicate with both the Indians and Pakistanis and took on cases of immigration, housing needs and equality in employment. He also provided race relations training to the police, community/social workers, and faith organisations. He was very much respected by all the communities because of his dedication and friendly nature which made a lot of difference in improving community and race relations. Even the Asian elders had no problem with their young people liaising with Narendra whose main consideration was what was good for the community.

As far as the AYO was concerned, its membership had grown, and it needed a place where they could gather and get involved in social activities and so they approached Narendra Sharma who understood the concerns and the dilemmas the youngsters were facing. He reassured them that he would do his best, through his contacts, to organise a meeting between them and the youth worker employed by the local government. After a week, Narendra asked the committee members to attend a meeting, which he had organised with the youth worker and so they all met. The youth worker agreed to look into it and asked the youths what they were looking to do at such a centre. The committee members told him that they wanted a place where they could gather and participate in social activities such as playing pool, and exercising, provide advice to the members regarding education, careers and give them the confidence to move forward in life. A week later, the community worker asked Narendra to organise another meeting with the young people and the community youth worker gave them the good news that the Council had agreed to provide a large building exclusively for the youths.

This was on the condition that they would have to meet the expenses of the running costs like heating, electricity and cleaning. The committee members excitedly accepted the offer and were so grateful to the community youth worker and Narendra for listening to them because, although the Asian community was in a position to provide a centre, the community leaders and parents felt that the youths would drift away from the Asian culture. However, the youths had other ideas. The AYO wrote in their policy documents that their aim was to save the youths from crime by involving

The Tripartite Community and the Generation Gap

them in social activities and, because the committee members consisted of students aspiring to become social workers and teachers, the leaders were looking to inspire its members to move forward with their careers. AYO also included in their policies respect for elders and support for the Asian community with problems of immigration, racial discrimination, and participation in cultural activities.

It was a most pleasant experience for the youngsters who, at last, felt that they belonged to a youth group with whom they could share their problems and get some help. They were successfully campaigning against extreme far right groups with the help of left-wing, socialist, revolutionary groups who also attracted a small number of Muslim youths to become members, but it was short-lived. The Muslim youth were not interested in adopting a left-wing Marxist philosophy because they believed that Islam was their way of life and were committed to preserving their faith and culture. They wanted to inspire the younger generations and train them to be good citizens by giving them a sense of direction and mission, in order to become a positive force for social change.

Narendra regularly guided the youths through their

problems, by referring them to appropriate organisations such as the social workers and youth workers. He further helped the parents with various problems facing the Asian community such as immigration and social welfare and other benefits. The AYO youth centre also paved the way for the young people to look beyond their community and participate with white youngsters in playing football and learning martial arts and some went out on the town. So, on the whole, the Asian community started coexisting along with other communities very well.

It was really unfortunate that racism was taking different forms. One day a couple of white youths walked into the first mosque built in Batley and placed a pig's head on the altar in the mosque whilst a few Muslims were offering prayers. This news quickly spread within the Muslim community and soon hundreds gathered outside the Mosque including members of the Dewsbury and Batley Asian Youth Organisation. The youngsters and older generations were shocked and angry, shouting 'we want justice.' Soon, the police arrived who tried to reassure the Muslims that they would find the people who were responsible, but the youths were not satisfied and told the police that if they could not

The Tripartite Community and the Generation Gap

find them, they would find them themselves. More people gathered and started marching towards the police station in Batley, about three miles away.

They continued asking for justice and chanted slogans against racism. When they reached the police station, the Chief Superintendent was waiting outside and asked to talk to the community leaders and the youth leaders. As the chanting against racism grew louder, he told them that he had already sent police to find the culprits who had left the pig's head and that they would be brought to justice. So, the Muslims demanded that the police stick to their word, and they would go home peacefully. Within a few hours, the police had arrested those who were responsible. They were freed on bail, but the Muslims were not satisfied, as they feared that repetitions might follow in future.

The news of the pig's head left in the mosque travelled around the country and more Muslims were ready to come to Batley to support the local Muslims. However, the local Muslim leaders, after having a meeting, advised them not to come, as the police had arrested those who were responsible. However, the members of the AYO demanded a meeting with the mosque leaders and, although the elders advised them to keep calm and let the police take the culprits to court, the youths organised a rally at the Dewsbury Town centre mosque, supported by a few elders and the mosque committee members. At the rally, some community leaders demanded that this kind of racist behaviour should not be allowed to be repeated. Whilst the youths were wanting to organise a vigilante group, fearing that more attacks might take place, the police chief who was present at the rally reassured them that he would put a police presence around all the mosques and the community, and they would do everything possible to prevent such racist behaviour. Finally, the youths listened to the elders and Narendra Sharma, for whom both the elders and youths had lots of respect. The police reassured them that justice would be done by taking legal action against those who left the pig's head and in the end the young people agreed not to organise a vigilante group and the outcome of this gathering was a harmonious one.

The Dewsbury and Batley Asian Youth Organisation continued to campaign against racism and prejudice till 1984. After that, it was dissolved as the members felt that the extreme right-wing organisations had slowly started withdrawing support from the local white people that the racist organisations had declined and that more chances for the young Asians in the field of employment were opening up due to the strict race relations laws against racial discrimination. Also, many succeeded with their education and became teachers, social workers, youth workers while others got apprenticeships in other skilled jobs such as plumbing, joinery, building trade mechanics, and the elders continued working in the very few remaining textile mills and as taxi drivers.

Some of the former AYO committee members started their local community newspaper called Awaaz (the voice) and continued to campaign against racial discrimination. For the first time, a couple of women brought up and educated here also joined Awaaz and wrote articles dealing with women's issues. The Awaaz group also gave practical help to those who needed services like interpretation and other community-related problems. All was done voluntarily. They also joined the Community Relations Council which was later replaced by the Commission for Racial Equality and a member of Awaaz was recruited along with a few others from the local Asian community to work towards improving

From the Splendid Sun to the Glorious Pound

race relations. Three members of the Awaaz group also became members of the local Racial Equality Committee and participated in improving community and race relations, the Committee also advised local government regarding the housing needs amongst the growing numbers of Asian families. Those who could not afford to buy a bigger house to cater for the growing children, were given grants by the local government to build extensions with a further bedroom, bathroom, and more space such as a larger kitchen and living room. These initiatives helped the Asians to continue living in an expanding but still close-knit community.

As far as the Asian youths were concerned, by the 1980s they were continuing to socialise with white youths and going out on the town, eating meals, and playing sports. Often the Asians, brought them home and treated them to authentic Asian food, the older white people also started loving Indian food which they used to frown upon in the past in the textile factories because they didn't have the opportunity to socialise with Asians, but now this was possible because the Asians started factories and trading and opening petrol stations and restaurants and takeaways

The Tripartite Community and the Generation Gap

outside their community. Ahmed bought a large semi-detached house and a Mercedes car. Similarly, those who were owners of petrol station businesses and bed factories started buying bigger houses and more luxurious cars. Those less well-off were buying second-hand cars like Ford and mostly Japanese cars, and those who did not have cars were given lifts when going shopping and to functions and the younger ones also took friends to movies and out in the town. So, like the white community, the Asians also started a working-class and middle-class system, quite different from the time when they all had similar status as textile workers, with similar houses and lifestyles.

The arranged marriage system continued amongst the Asian community even though many youngsters were educated and brought up here. The old traditions of keeping it in the family from the village days continued. Some were not happy with this but had little choice, because the women were not allowed go into further education and the men had no chance to meet them, so the elder in the community would volunteer to bring marriage proposals. Most young Muslims lived near their parents, so the tradition of parental support continued. Many younger men continued socialising with friends from school, college and work and enjoyed life outside the community, whilst the grandparents helped by caring for their grandchildren. A few youngsters even got married to partners from the white community even if the parents did not approve. They set up a separate nuclear family life outside the community and most were happy, apart from a few who could not cope with the cultural differences, and they were helped by the moral support of some former members of the old AYO. Within a couple of years, the Asian community were living in a comfort zone and were able to go about their daily lives without being physically attacked by the extreme right-wing party members and individuals. Young Muslims were moving up the social mobility ladder, and the majority of people in the community were not facing growing poverty, but living comfortable lifestyles and, like their parents, were not afraid to work long and unsociable hours. Being brought up with such traditions was a real asset for them.

Councils that did not employ many Asians were investigated by the Commission for Racial Equality and recommendations were made to the government that these local authorities must employ Black people and Asians to

The Tripartite Community and the Generation Gap

create balance and so the council got funding from central government under 'Section Eleven.' It helped to train and employ people from ethnic minorities and, as a result, many got jobs in the Council. Also, one of the former member of the Asian Youth Organisation with a Hindu background joined the police force and remained there for many years and was promoted to a superintendent. Being Asian and speaking Hindi and Urdu, he made a real difference to the police department as there were hardly any Asians in the police force. He made a career for himself and was promoted to Sergeant level. There was another former chairman of the Asian Youth Organisation who tirelessly worked towards campaigning for racial equality, particularly for the youth. He later went to study law as a mature student and worked for a couple of law firms for a few years before opening his own practice where he successfully dealt with many criminal cases. The education department even funded a new initiative, a course known as an 'Access course' at Dewsbury and Batley College, where those Asians who had missed further education were able to study for one year as mature students. In this way, they would qualify for further education at a university and become professionals, which also allowed them to work for Kirklees Metropolitan Council. Overall, the Asians started to become part of the mainstream British economic and social institutions.

On the religious front, the committee at the Markaz built a madrasa attached to the Markaz which attracted students locally as well as from around the country. The mosque and the new madrasa were self-financed by the community and the students only paid the costs of their education and accommodation. The idea behind the religious education and building of the mosque was the philosophy that Muslims must become pious and learn about Islamic behaviour, how to live a dignified and moral life without causing disharmony amongst themselves or amongst the indigenous population. They maintained the idea that most of the white people were friendly and tolerant, and the Muslims must show appreciation and behave well towards them. However, even though things were looking up for the Asians, something else was lying in wait in Dewsbury. Unfortunately, there were a few ignorant local whites who, without looking closely at the lifestyle of the Muslims, decided to campaign against the Muslim community for creating a private religious school.

Over the months in early 1989, an increasing number of

The Tripartite Community and the Generation Gap

white parents in the Savile Town area withdrew their children from the local school, which had become 80 per cent Asian. In June, the Extreme Right-wing Party organised a rally to support these parents, whose behaviour was both in the media and illegal under English and Welsh law. The rally, in the centre of Dewsbury, was met with a small group of counter-demonstrators from Kirklees Black Workers' Association, but later, a group of around 800 Asians gathered. Heavy-handed policing forced the group of Asians back to Savile Town, the Asian area, which led to fighting and the burning down of the Scarborough pub in the area. Many Asian market holders in the centre of Dewsbury reported that they were abused by the Extreme Right-Wing activists, since the police were diverted to Savile Town. Fifty-eight people were arrested, most of whom were Asian, and prison sentences ranged from three months to three years. Two police officers were injured.

From the Splendid Sun to the Glorious Pound

CHAPTER TEN

Children of Vision

Around 1986, the second- generation Muslims gradually found their identity as British Indian Muslims or British Pakistani Muslims. Their dreams and ambitions were beyond the traditional village culture and their life was constantly improving. Their elders had established a community life similar to the villages back home where everyone knew everyone, shared common goals, and supported each other but they also had to get used to living a regimented lifestyle, where the clock dictated their daily routines. They found this rather difficult, when back home they lived a more relaxed lifestyle in villages, where they were able to come whenever they wanted to from the farms and used to sleep during the afternoon and woke up to masala Indian tea and got back to the farm to work but being victims of poverty was unbearable. Here, one thing both generations had in common was that any kind of division was almost impossible as far as the common goal of living as a family went.

The younger generations had the vision to adopt a

combined culture, by incorporating some of the indigenous culture along with the Asian culture. This presented challenging tasks of pleasing both communities, but most importantly they wanted to please themselves and achieve higher social mobility, either by education or learning practical employment skills, funded by the government job creation schemes, or by being self-employed, and they did well. Their aspirations for a better future were further helped by the 1976 Race Relations Act established by the British government to prevent discrimination on the grounds of race, colour, nationality, ethnic and national origin in the field of employment, provision of goods and services, education and public functions.

The second generation of Asians also joined the Indian Muslim Welfare Society which included some former members of the local Asian Youth Organisation. When these youngsters became parents, many were already working as social workers, community youth workers and teachers. Many others were already working for local government departments, thinking of new initiatives to further advance the functions of the Indian Muslim Welfare Society, to serve the changing Muslim community and to raise funds from government community grant systems. Their efforts funded the purchase of a large building in Batley in the heart of the Muslim community which would facilitate various community and religious functions. The organisation had the added benefit of one former supporter of the Asian Youth Organisation who had graduated with a degree. He had extensive experience in raising grants for community organisations, which made him instrumental in securing grants for the centre. The centre was called the Al-Hikmah Centre to promote religious harmony between different religious communities living locally and nationally and to positively promote Islam, advancing education and employment opportunities and providing and facilitating training for the local community and promoting such other charitable purposes as may from time to time be determined. Here they had a large sports hall, two large halls for social events and conferences, and a separate building that had seminar rooms, prayer rooms and training centres.

Racism continued throughout the UK, but the physical attacks had decreased, and more Asians and whites were now interacting through businesses and socialising. There were growing numbers of taxi drivers mostly providing services to the white community, such as to shoppers, hospital visits, picking up those who went out on the town to pubs and clubs and Indian restaurants and on the way, they might exchange jokes and entertain each other. Some Asian taxi drivers started wearing Islamic clothes and would attend mosques to perform prayers, so this kind of co-existence culture was developing, and it worked for both communities, occasionally taxi drivers were still physically attacked by some racists, but that did not deter the Asians from earning a living this way. Within the last twenty years much has been written about the Asian community and questions asked by the media, politicians and social scientists analysing the behavioural aspects of the Asian community trying to determine how best they can be helped to be part of the British culture. They came up with several terminologies such as should Asians be encouraged to move towards 'assimilation,' 'integration' or 'coexistence'?

Some of the conservative media, government and many from the indigenous community believed that the Asians were not integrating, but this view was based on their biased thinking, rather than an attempt to understand the reality of the situation, such as how much the Asians had to struggle

Children of Vision

and suffer and they had no other alternatives than to form their own close-knit community, together with working long and unsociable hours which didn't give them any time to look beyond their community. Once a taxi driver was talking to a white passenger, who told him 'That he was doing a good job taking him to the pub, but he could not understand why the Asians do not go to the pubs and clubs and socialise a bit to help race relations. The taxi driver replied, 'It is against their religion to do that and anyway the Asians are too busy working long, unsociable hours and helping the British way of life by taking them to pubs, clubs, running takeaways, restaurants, and corner shops.' To which the passenger said 'Now I understand. It is a hard life mate.

At the time when the Asians were settling in and struggling to come to terms with their changing lifestyle and family responsibilities, the last thing they wanted to hear was academics, politicians and the media in the UK apply terminologies and analyse their behaviours. However, it was just coincidence that traditionally the Asians chose to live amongst themselves and by looking after their affairs and respecting the white people and their culture. Therefore, this can be considered as co-existence, which is unlikely to change in the near future, simply because the younger Asians have also taken exception to these kinds of sociological and psychological analyses, and it has further reinforced their determination to live within the close-knit Asian community. Similarly, Asians of various religious backgrounds established close-knit communities across the country, including different parts of London, Birmingham, Leicester, Blackburn, Glasgow, and many other towns and cities. In Dewsbury and Batley, the Community Relations Council was replaced with Commission for the Racial Equality amalgamated with the National Racial Equality Councils, with different functions in light of the changes in communities with more youngsters being born and brought up in the UK. There was a need for them to address such issues by promoting equality of opportunity and so they established employment officers to promote equal rights for the Asians and Black people accordingly.

The second-generation Asians continued to adopt an East-West culture, showing a keen interest in artists like Michael Jackson, Prince, Madonna, Duran Duran, and Wham. They also went to movies such as Star Wars and watched TV favourites like Dynasty, Dallas, and new soap operas from Australia. The launch of MTV and its music videos further dominated Britain's pop culture scene, and the Asian youth eagerly joined in the trend. Top of The Pops on the TV had some influences on the youth, some even imitated their favourite popstars with similar hairstyles and clothes, particularly Elvis Presley, whereas the majority of youngsters continued with their own chosen lifestyle. The Asian community so far had led a happy cultural and religious life, but success comes with a price and although small in numbers, divorce rates increased, and psychological problems started occurring too. It was apparent that big cracks were appearing in the Asian community, whilst they thought they were having such a harmonious lifestyle.

Divorce rates slowly began increasing and were more common amongst those who were married to partners from the Indian subcontinent. Whilst many accepted the marriage and made it work, some were brought up in the UK and had a problem relating to their husbands or wives who could not speak English and so could not share the same sense of humour. In some cases, they displayed controlling behaviour because they believed that their spouse should obey them. For those who were brought up in the UK, the marriages survived with moral and financial support from parents. Also, the majority of wives were better placed to understand the children who were born here and who were more inclined to listen to their mother rather than father, because the father was from India and Pakistan and did not understand the children's culture of growing up here and so they left it to their wives to bring the children up and educate them. It was a happy arrangement the husband being the breadwinner and wives taking on the domestic responsibilities. On the educational front, many young Asians continued to go into further education, and they were further supported by their parents who kept on reminding them not to work in the textile factories, but most of the mills had closed anyway, due to competition from abroad.

The majority of young Asians normally chose subjects such as sciences because the Asians also had a tradition of working in the British National Health Service as doctors and in other occupations. Many who started going for further education at university had already qualified in degrees such as physiology, biochemistry, pharmacists, others with degrees in economics, commerce, business studies and law, but they chose careers in business, either working in supermarkets or starting their own businesses, and only a few changed direction towards working as a social worker, teachers, drivers, joiners, electricians, motor mechanics and in catering. Many parents had either retired or were unemployed and many, after going on pilgrimage to Makkah in Saudi Arabia, felt satisfied that their adventure of migrating to the UK and all the hard work had paid off and it was time to spend time with extended families and live a pious religious life. They were satisfied with the money they had saved up and lived in comfortable houses. Many children continued living with their parents, including a few who were married and were earning enough to look after families as well as parents. Also, living as an extended family everyone was a winner and lived in comfort.

The second generation of Asians had different challenges ahead compared with those of their parents: lifestyle changes, going abroad on holiday, better housing, cars, eating out in restaurants, and going out shopping in shopping centres and retail parks. A few Asian supermarkets and shops were opening where food from around the world with different varieties was available, such as spices, lentils, different types of flour for chapatis and naan, rice, pickles, and sweets with more choice than back in the Indian subcontinent, and plenty of it at prices they could afford. The youngsters would benefit from the traditional Asian dishes as well as English and foreign dishes as their eating habits started to change. They would enjoy pizzas, middle eastern foods such as doner kebabs, western foods, including fish and chips, even English food once considered 'bland' was now being cooked at home.

As far as entertainment was concerned, British TV started casting more Asians but still stereotypes of roles such as 'Mr Patel' the owner of a corner shop or 'Mr Khan' the owner of a takeaway. Bollywood movies and Pakistani dramas in Urdu continued to dominate Asian cultures because by now growing numbers of television programmes from the Indian subcontinent were being viewed through satellite and cable TV, including news and cooking programmes, which the parents enjoyed very much, particularly the traditional women who did not go out much and enjoyed such programmes. The youngsters brought up here continued watching British soaps, football, documentaries, and news. Whilst all these changes were taking place, many more mosques were established, and more Muslims started turning towards their faith. At the same time, the women started driving cars, the well-to-do husbands would buy cars and the young women who were working contributed towards the domestic bills, holidays, and cars. Children also started enjoying expensive toys, designer clothes and were given private tuition so that they had a better chance of going to university.

After a few years of experiencing higher social mobility, nuclear families within the Asian community began moving out of their closed enclaves and into detached or semi-detached houses with larger gardens. Despite this shift, many parents chose to stay in their old homes, which they had purchased in the 1960s and 1970s, a symbol of their pride in their achievements in coming to the UK. As the community grew by the thousands, the demand for more mosques and madrasas increased. Fortunately, this was not much of a problem, as other prosperous Muslim communities throughout the UK were able to provide financial contributions to support the religious institutions. Thanks to their determination to sustain their religion and culture, the Asian elders were able to benefit from National Insurance pensions and support from their children, affording them a comfortable retirement. They continued to live a simple, traditional lifestyle and were content with their financial arrangements, enabling them to travel back home for holidays and make pilgrimages to Makkah in Saudi Arabia. Many still lived as part of extended families, enjoying the added benefit of spending time with their grandchildren.

Meanwhile, the number of second-generation Asians continued to grow, and many were making progress up the career ladder, even venturing outside their community to work in neighbouring towns and cities. With this new-found prosperity, they began buying better houses, setting up new businesses such as bed factories, petrol stations, pharmacies, and market stalls. Asian wives also entered the workforce, taking on roles in high street shops, local authorities, schools as teachers, lawyers, and even as beauticians. The new-found prosperity also encouraged these families to invest more in their children's education, providing private tuition to help them achieve even greater success. Many also started to marry according to their own choices by meeting partners at work or at weddings for example and many also accepted that their parents and relatives might find the right match with someone who had been born and educated here with similar educational and cultural backgrounds, and they had the right to refuse if they were not happy with such an arrangement.

The status of Muslims started changing with better education, jobs, and a better quality of life. They became joint decision-makers as to how the functions of the families should be carried out. However, there were challenges in maintaining such lifestyles and the changes meant that it became more stressful and because of work there was not enough time to spend with the children and so there was the risk of the family being less together, which was the tradition up to now. There was more income, but a changing lifestyle meant more financial burdens for having this materialistic life, which started creating individualism. In Western societies, these kinds of changes had taken place gradually over many years, whereas with the Asians it was happening so quickly over just twenty years. Also, it created class differences amongst the Asians, with the affluent people having better homes, cars and other material needs and others still living in terrace houses bought by parents. It was based on earnings and materialism, but the better off continued to give financial loans and assist relatives and friends by giving them loans with no interest to buy houses and other domestic requirements.

They also gave huge sums of money towards the building and running of mosques and madrasas, including supporting the poor back in the villages. This was based on the religious philosophy that if you are better off, then it is your duty to help relatives, neighbours, and friends. The Asian community maintained the idea that if they were to stay in the UK indefinitely, they must continue to instil positivity into their children so that they can continue living prosperous lifestyles, and to do this they would borrow ideas from other parents whose children were role models, who were already doing well and this encouraged their children, and it was all done for the good of the community. Also, successive British governments continued to encourage and assist the communities by training careers officers to provide career guidance.

The Indian and Pakistani communities were well settled by now and were having more faith in the British people and the government, their life expectancies were increasing compared to people in India and Pakistan and, despite missing the good weather, the village life and the social life,

Children of Vision

they were doing better here than they had expected and in return, they contributed towards the British economy and lifestyle by working and being respectable citizens, so much so that they would not be looking to settle back in India or Pakistan permanently. Here they were happy and visited family and friends and shared common interests and formed a close-knit community like the villages in India and Pakistan. They remained happy and it was almost like continuous celebrations for their brilliant life in Britain.

Many elders continued to retain dual nationalities, both Pakistani and British. However, at the same time, mostly the first and some of the second generations had visited relatives back at home and were able to catch up on what they missed. It became the custom for them to select the months when there are plenty of tropical fruits available, particularly mangoes and with a sense of humour, they would say that they were 'going for the mangoes. Furthermore, because of the British currency rates, they got more rupees to the British pound, and they were able to treat their relatives with food, clothing and were able to go on tours and enjoy the sunshine. The children from the UK also had the opportunity to meet grandparents and relatives and learn about the traditional village cultures. The British citizens would tell their relatives in India and Pakistan stories about their struggles and challenges in the UK and what they had achieved. They spoke highly of the successive British governments and the white people.

Here in the UK, many Asians gradually started moving away from the terrace houses to nearby affluent areas with detached and semi-detached houses and big gardens. However, as Asians started moving into the white areas, some white neighbours started moving out, although others stayed for longer. There was a dilemma as the majority of well-to-do Muslims, once again started moving out of the traditional closed community settings and to more middle-class areas and started forming an affluent middle class close-knit Asian community, whilst many elders stayed in their traditional settings. These middle-class Asians were willing to pay the white neighbours more than the market value for their houses and, although they liked the Asians, the white neighbours were benefiting from the lucrative selling prices and were able to buy better and bigger houses in other white areas, in other towns or villages and so perhaps it was not all due to racism that the white people were moving out, but was more to do with economic reasons, so to be fair to them they can't be branded as racists.

As far as both communities were concerned, there were no ulterior motives other than to live a comfortable lifestyle, according to their choice, but was taken by some of the conservative media, some white people, and a few members of the government as evidence that Asians did not want to integrate. However, Asians ignored these examples of unfounded accusations because they knew that they were positively contributing to British society by working hard and paying taxes. They did not have any feelings of guilt and continued with their traditions of enjoying the community life. By now they had a taste for a more contemporary lifestyle with more modern housing, matching furniture, washing machines, large American-style fridge freezers, stylish modern baths and showers, going out for meals and driving modern cars. They wore fashionable western clothes, some girls even wore jeans and other western fashion clothes, but in moderation and at the same time. The number of pious Muslims grew as they felt that, after overcoming poverty, their life was not complete without faith if they wanted to have a successful community and family life.

Around the 1960s back at home in India and Pakistan, people were the victims of poverty where their income was insufficient for their basic needs and where every rupee had to be spent wisely. It was a hand-to-mouth situation. Even after a few years of being in the UK life was not that brilliant for some as they were still struggling whilst settling here but compared to back home, the life here was still better. Now after being here for the last thirty years or so, families were earning enough to buy necessities. People did have to earn more to sustain the demanding materialistic lifestyle, which meant more demands on the families. By now, the changes in the status of Muslim women made a huge difference and the percentage of women in employment kept growing. They were earning salaries as ordinary workers and professionals due to having education, some to degree levels, and this added extra income for the family.

The menfolk who were the traditional breadwinners while the women who stayed at home were replaced by husbands and wives sharing the costs of running a house and contributing together towards maintaining a good family life and decision making. The traditional culture of arranged marriages was replaced by youngsters choosing their partners and getting married, which was quite easy now that often both individuals were born and educated in the UK, sharing the quality of family life according to their own choice. The concept of people from the community helping to find partners for marrying still exists but with the consent of both partners after being introduced and getting to know each other before getting married, and the traditional parents by now have realised the importance of considering the children's choice. It was getting easier for Asians to climb the economic ladder due to obstacles such as racism having been removed or reduced. In addition, the government and educational institutions had accepted the idea that the second and third generations of Asians were more than capable of competing in education and careers, which all led to increasing numbers of people moving away from a corner shop or takeaway business to better-paid employment.

The Asian community was becoming more assimilated with the British culture, and they saw a bright future for their children. As they became more prosperous, they moved away from the traditional extended family model and started living as nuclear families. This meant taking on more responsibilities for their own children, instead of relying on the moral and financial support of their parents and other extended family members. The more prosperous Muslims began going on holiday abroad to places like Dubai, Turkey, Morocco, Jordan, Malaysia and Egypt, where they could enjoy the warm weather and the Islamic culture. The elders also began building new houses in India and Pakistan and sending money to their poorer relatives. However, the second and third generations did not see India and Pakistan as their home, and although they visited there for holidays and enjoyed it, they felt homesick and preferred the lifestyle in the UK. The status of Muslims began to change as they gained better education, jobs, and a higher quality of life, leading to joint decision-making within families. However, the changes in lifestyle also brought stress and less time to spend with children, potentially leading to a decline in the tradition of togetherness. Despite the increase in income, materialism created a risk of individualism and class differences, with affluent individuals having better homes and possessions than others who still lived in the terrace houses bought by their parents.

However, the better off members of the community

Children of Vision

continued to provide financial support to their relatives and friends, offering interest-free loans to buy houses and assisting with other domestic needs. They also donated large sums of money towards building and running mosques and madrasas, as well as supporting the poor in their villages, guided by their religious philosophy. The Asian community remained determined to maintain a positive outlook for their children's future prosperity in the UK, seeking inspiration from successful role models and sharing ideas among parents. Successive British Governments have also assisted the community by training career officers to provide career guidance. However, the changes in lifestyle and materialism emphasized the importance of instilling strong values of togetherness, family, and community, to prevent the loss of these traditions amidst the evolving landscape.

The Indian and Pakistani communities were well settled by now and were having more faith in the British people and the government, their life expectancies were increasing compared to India and Pakistan and despite missing the good weather the village life and the social life, they were doing better here than they had bargained for and in return, they contributed towards the British economy and lifestyle by working and being respectable citizens, so much so that they were not looking to go back to settle in India or Pakistan permanently. Here they were happy and visited family and friends and shared common interests and formed a close-knit community like the villages in India and Pakistan.

The relatives back at home were attracted to the idea of coming to the UK too and if that was not possible, they continued to request that their children should be invited to the UK to marry and settle permanently, but by now there were growing mixed feelings amongst some of the Asians in the UK as they had difficulties in persuading their children to marry in India and Pakistan. This quite often created conflict and the relatives back home got upset and made the British citizens feel guilty for not honouring the original relationships at a time when they were all one family, but all was not lost because the UK citizens either renovated the old family houses or built new ones there with more contemporary styles and the relatives would enjoy living in comfort. They would also utilise farms belonging to the British Citizens free of charge for looking after them.

Chapter Eleven

Changes in Fortune

Third-generation Asians took an objective view of the concept of arranged marriages and the tradition of 'keeping it within the family.' They refused to marry cousins or close family as they believed that it was wrong to marry someone with whom they had grown up in an extended family. They realised that marrying cousins could lead to inherited diseases such as Thalassaemia or sickle cell disease. In Batley, Yorkshire, the Health department commissioned a Muslim health professional to make a film based on an actual case study. A brother's son married his sister's daughter and cases of Thalassaemia followed. When their doctor tried to explain the problems of marrying inside the family, it created conflict and the boy's father who was more of a traditionalist and conservative got terribly upset with the brother-in-law. He also accused the health department of interfering with their religion and traditions, claiming that such transactions had been practised for hundreds of years and as far as he was concerned there was nothing wrong in marrying within the close family.

From the Splendid Sun to the Glorious Pound

The wedding ceremony itself also took on a new look as the youth culture now meant lavish weddings parties, where hundreds, and in some cases, thousands of people attended a wedding and enjoyed quality food. The youngsters would hire Hollywood-style limousines, wear Bollywood-style designer clothes and have fireworks. Families and friends would go to the wedding houses two weeks before the wedding day and sit in a marquee with a Moroccan, Indian or Pakistani theme and enjoy delicious food, fun and laughter. New traditions emerged, inspired by the white community, such as the popular stag night, where male friends and family members would gather to celebrate and play light-hearted pranks on the groom-to-be. The womenfolk would have hen nights, just for women and would play pranks on the bride.

A day before the wedding, they would organise a mehndi (henna) party, a tradition from back home where mainly women gathered and hired a henna artist to put henna on the women's hands. Applying mehndi with its artistically designed patterns takes a long time and they put on Indian or Pakistani music and people would dance, and everyone behaved in a festive mood. The menfolk, members of the extended family and friends would slip through the net and would share the delicious food, which was different to the wedding food, being more like the traditional street food of home. Before the wedding day, it became customary for the bride with her women friends and relatives to go for a long walk every day for a month, so that they would lose weight and be able to wear the clothes and look slimmer. All these factors were symptomatic of the changing culture, now based on properties and materialism. On the wedding day itself, celebrations took place in Banquets and other venues built expressly for wedding celebrations. They would hire professionals to design Bollywood-style colourful stages, so the wedding venue provided a beautiful background for the romantically-styled interiors, and instead of the guests eating at a long table as happened in the past, the younger generation would insist on having round tables so that families could have their own tables to socialise and enjoy the celebrations. The family guests would buy expensive presents but sometimes, as a newly-adopted custom for some, the bride and groom would put a request 'no gift boxes please' on the wedding invitation cards to prevent multiples of the same gift. It is not customary to tell the guests to give certain gifts or ask them to choose something

From the Splendid Sun to the Glorious Pound

from a list. There were added benefits to receiving cash gifts as they helped towards the cost of the wedding. The happy couple would then go on a honeymoon abroad, mostly in countries like Dubai, Morocco, Tunisia, or Turkey, because of the nice weather, halal food and similar Islamic cultures. Many of the elders, who had come through a history of struggle and challenges, did not approve of the youngsters moving away from the traditions of simplicity to spend lavishly on weddings, but they had no choice. They took comfort from the fact that the younger generation did, at least, believe in the concept of marriage rather than just living together as partners, without performing an Islamic marriage. On the other hand, there were those Muslims who lived a simple Islamic life, invited limited amounts of guests, and continued to marry without lavish wedding expenses. Instead, they gave money to charities.

Here, those who were practising Muslims also took some comfort from seeing that what had begun as a small faith community in Dewsbury and Batley was growing even larger in numbers and many young Muslims were becoming practising Muslims and started growing beards and wore Islamic clothes. Growing numbers of young women were also becoming devoted to their faith. The Asians did not abandon the traditional culture of living with strong family and social and community interactions and were living happily rather than living in small families on their own away from the community and becoming socially isolated, particularly in old age. But as time passed, this started changing.

The Asians were able to feel even more British and were reassuring themselves that the future was looking very bright for future generations. Their changing lifestyles meant that they had to get large mortgages, and some were already breaking away from the tradition of being a part of extended families. Nevertheless, these were still in small numbers and the majority preferred to live with extended families. Those youngsters who started living as a nuclear family, with just husband, wife, and children, entailed more responsibilities in caring for the children. In the past, the extended family had provided moral and financial support. and if not living in one household they would live in the same neighbourhoods. By now, many who had come from back home had built new houses in India and Pakistan and sent money to poor relatives, but the second and third generations did not entertain such ideas and no longer regarded India and Pakistan as home. They did, however, enjoy the holidays in those countries but after a few weeks, they felt homesick and returned to the UK.

As the community was becoming more affluent, so the need for spending more money on the religious and cultural requirements increased, and more mosques were being built with larger facilities to cater for the growing Muslim community. Now, the people had no problems financing the building of larger mosques and madrasas. Now, mosque committees did not have to go door to door to collect a few pounds as they did in the 60s and 70s around the UK. The more prosperous Muslims gave large sums of money. Also, as far as the madrasas were concerned, they were self-financing because of the fees paid by parents for their children's religious education. Increasing numbers of youngsters born and brought up in the UK, were being trained to become either a Hafiz (a person who memorised the Quran by heart) or a Maulana (A religious scholars). They had an added advantage because they were fluent in the English language, like the majority of young people they spoke the Yorkshire dialect and so were better placed to

Changes in Fortune

teach the children born in the UK.

When someone completes their religious studies to become a Hafiz or Maulana, a special ceremony is usually organised by the mosque to honour their achievement. During the ceremony, the students are expected to recite the Quran and are presented with certificates and gifts. The family of the student may then host social and religious events to celebrate this accomplishment, often renting a venue similar to those used for weddings. Meals are served, and guests typically give monetary gifts to the student as a token of their congratulations. Speeches are made by community leaders and scholars, wishing the newly-qualified student the best of luck and requesting them to serve the community by teaching others and being respectable citizens. Later on, women also qualified to become Alimas, and Hafiz is taught separately by women scholars. They are given the same ceremony as the men, and they are also expected to teach other female students. This kind of achievement is possible because they live in such a close-knit community.

The younger generations also brought new changes to the way they ate and moved further from the traditional foods. They started eating American-style burgers, Turkish doner kebabs and English food such as sandwiches, and even started cooking English and Italian meals at home. At Christmas, some Muslims would buy halal turkeys from Muslim butchers and some even made Indian-style marinated masala chickens and others cooked Christmas dinners which would be enjoyed as family meals but only as a social event without any religious significance. They give presents to white neighbours and socialise with them, and the white neighbours also give the Asians presents. Whilst all these social changes were part of growing up in the UK, the one thing that remained in their minds was to keep the Islamic faith and plan life accordingly.

As far as entertainment was concerned, this was a happy time for the Asian community - they grew up to be more confident and they felt that the struggle that their parents and grandparents had to face in the early stages, will never be repeated. Adding to their excitement, the entertainment industry also began to produce sitcoms incorporating the traditional British Asian culture and modern British life. The BBC, for example started showing a comedy series 'Goodness Gracious Me,' an English language comedy with different sketches and characters, televised from 1998. The cast consisted of British Asian actors and the show explored British Asian culture and the conflicts and integration issues between traditional South Asian culture, and the modern British life of South Asian culture. Some sketches were examined from the Asian perspective and others made fun of the Asian stereotypes overall. The programmes were well received by audiences from different backgrounds. Also, after the British Actors Equity's equality committee campaign for integrated casting, more Asian, Black, and Chinese actors were given roles in British soaps and other dramas.

As with every success in life, there are downsides to it as well. Back home, poverty, disease and lack of proper healthy food meant that life expectancies were low, whereas in the UK there is the better, free health system, education, money to spend on quality foods and material goods, but due to unhealthy eating, diabetes and heart conditions have increased in South Asians compared to the white population. Food is the most important part of Asian social gatherings, as they preserve cultural ties similar to back home in India and Pakistan. It is considered bad mannered to turn down certain foods and so the dietary requirement for keeping weight down is a real struggle within a large community and families where there are frequent social functions. People find the lure of freshly prepared authentic Indian and Pakistani dishes almost impossible to resist but they have no control over how it was prepared. It is considered inhospitable to offer curries with fewer spices or oil and some people even request a bit more oil on their plates, being traditionally of the opinion that butter, milk, and oil are more nutritious. Indian food has become part of a British tradition and white guests who are used to eating Indian food by now, also compliment the hosts for serving such tasty dishes.

As far as politics is concerned, Asian councillors are being elected throughout the UK, including in Dewsbury and Batley, and although they are mostly from the Labour Party, there are others from the Conservatives and Liberal Democrats. There are also a few Asian MPs, which is evidence that the Asians are being taken seriously by the political parties, and they pride themselves on having a voice in politics. However, the percentage of Asians going into mainstream politics is still extremely low as they are still concentrating more on business than in the past, in order to

Changes in Fortune

have a secure future. They continue to support each other by branching out into different business activities such as owning pharmacies, running petrol stations with mini supermarkets, opening more restaurants and takeaways, garages, construction, investing in properties to rent, working in banks, opening post offices, and buying carpet and furniture stores. Having economic independence means a better quality of life, so politics is not a priority. In fact, very few people study politics: mostly they are attracted to sciences or business studies or training in practical skills, such as plumbers, electricians, or motor mechanics. However, those who did realise the importance of how politics affected their lives and supported both white and Asian candidates, but the Asians realised that their interests would be better served by electing an Asian candidate. For this reason, the community leaders took active parts by persuading their community to vote, and they would campaign for the Labour Party as their parents did traditionally, and within a few years, the percentage of Asians taking active parts in politics grew, and the numbers of the Asian Councillors from different political parties had been elected.

From the Splendid Sun to the Glorious Pound

Ever since they came to the UK, Asians have had to face many challenges and difficulties to achieve the real benefits of their migration, but at the same time they did not forget their extended family members and the village communities back home who they supported in the past. Their efforts did not go to waste because they started earning money from India as well. Many had inherited land from their parents and, including what was left by their grandparents, the names of the first and the second generations of Indians who were born in India were listed on the land registry in India, and using modern technology this was easily put on computers, so their relatives were not able to sell the lands and properties. Many have invited the relatives from the UK to share it out among the family as the price of land was increasing. The UK family members went back to sort out the legal procedures, and either improved the existing houses or demolished them and built new ones They sold their share of the land to the members of their extended families or investors from other areas and brought the cash back to the UK. This was a real gift for the migrants who had never envisaged that the village, which was once so poor, would earn them money because the demand for the houses and

Changes in Fortune

land made them valuable and profitable.

However, in some cases, it also created conflict with relatives in India and legal action had to be taken by people from the UK. They would go to India personally, hire a legal team and normally they would win the case. Sometimes, they had to pay off the relatives to remove their names from the land registry. In some cases, this also made them fall out with the relatives back at home, but it did not affect them much as they were unlikely to want to go back and live there permanently. Most of the parents had passed away and those remaining were taken care of by the family members. The family from the UK would send money for their keep. Ultimately, both families, there and in the UK, were happy.

As time passed, the third generation of Asians who were born and grew up in the UK started losing their traditional Asian languages, and so few would talk to their parents in their native language. However, among brothers, sisters, and friends, they would speak in English with Yorkshire dialects. Those whose parents either came at a young age from India or Pakistan and were educated here, or were born here, would speak to their children in English, because they were better placed to guide their children in education and careers compared to the parents who were not brought up here. They were struggling to guide their children and so got help from others who were educated here, who would advise and guide them. The parents had one thing in common which was to educate their children for better prospects. As a result, many youngsters succeeded in moving up the economic and social ladders.

The younger generations were becoming career-minded including the women and they did not entertain the idea of getting married earlier and waiting to secure their future. In fact, many youngsters found their partners by meeting them at their workplaces or universities or through the internet. Also, the idea of moving away from the parents after marriage became the norm and was not frowned upon by the community, because by now they have accepted the generation gap and the changing youth culture. The young people bought houses slightly away from the traditional, close community but kept their parents with them so the parents could live a comfortable life. Asians, particularly Muslims, were more family and community-oriented, children had more respect for their elders and took care of ageing parents in their own homes in the same town and neighbourhood. The children also benefited from the moral and financial support from their elders and in very few cases if the parents were not looked after, the social services would provide for their welfare.

Bashir had retired by now along with his many relatives and friends and his son Ahmed was doing well with his business. His daughter qualified and worked in health and beauty, and the son became an accountant. Musa and Jameela had three children: one son became a pharmacist, his second son studied at the Islamic School, training to be a Maulana and his daughter studied to become a teacher.

The culture of supporting each other remains the most important facet of community life. Helping at weddings, visiting the sick and providing food for them, helping at funerals by visiting and comforting the deceased family - neighbours and relatives would take food for about a week and eat with them. The culture of lending money for houses has remained, and some even buy houses by getting private loans from the sellers and pay the rest at a certain agreed time. Social life has also continued to improve with better employment and increasing numbers of the young generation taking an interest in sports, such as playing football and supporting their favourite teams, together with playing snooker and golf. Traditionally, the parents used to play cricket, but for the third generation, this has declined slowly.

Not everything is rosy though, because at the same time as the success stories, others are suffering from poverty due to lack of education and employment, having to do unskilled jobs which are not highly paid but compared to back home they enjoy a reasonably healthy and long happy lifestyle. Also, there are those parents who worked awfully hard, but lost their authority over their children and were not successful in guiding their children as far as education and careers were concerned. As a result, their children, although they are in the minority, started indulging in criminal activities such as taking or dealing in drugs or being in gangs. There are rising cases of young men going to prison or suffering from mental and other forms of illness due to these kinds of activities. It is very unfortunate because, like others, these families also came to Britain to pave the way for a better future for their children but were caught in a tangled web.

CHAPTER TWELVE

Wealth and Social Divides

As the Asian population grew after 1995, so did the economic divisions and, although the Muslim population remained at its core a close-knit community based on religion and cultural values, the community was splitting into different classes which was in complete contrast to the time when they worked in factories. There were people who continued leading a similar lifestyle and standard of living with small to medium terrace houses, in some cases overcrowded with large families. In fact, most Asians remained part of the working class, whereas the well-to-do professional people lived in larger, detached, or semi-detached houses and formed their own community, within the community overall but slightly away from the traditional community, where they interacted with people with similar interests and cultural values, based on a middle-class status.

In India and Pakistan, people of a lower class, a different sect and the poor were not looked upon favourably when it came to marriage, as those with a higher status believed that it was not good for their reputation. Whereas, in the UK, they had no problem with marriageable status, whether they were from poor working classes or upper and middle classes because they realised that the only way to get the children married was with freedom of choice. Finally, the youngsters had the freedom to choose the partner with whom they wished to spend the rest of their life. Many less well-to-do people had to struggle to survive on a single wage. Housewives who were less educated or lacked English language skills often came to the UK after marriage, without formal qualifications. To help make ends meet, they worked from home preparing samosas, chapatis, and other savouries, which they sold to restaurants and takeaways. This provided a valuable source of income to contribute towards household expenses and pay for their children's education. Also, because the divorce rate started increasing the single mothers also benefited by working in catering.

By now, Bashir's wife Amina had established her family business so well that she had bought a small warehouse and converted it into a catering business along with Jameela her daughter and Farida's daughter-in-law. They continued to employ other women and supplied food for restaurants, takeaways and weddings and other social events, as well as to

Wealth and Social Divides

shops, and petrol stations. However, Amina was getting old and the daughter and daughter-in-law managed the business, with the support of Ahmed who dealt with her finance.

The unemployment amongst the population in Dewsbury and Batley remained high due to the collapse of the textile industry and so it was exceedingly difficult for them to cope with the resulting poverty. Thankfully, the Asian businesses continued to invest in other businesses and gradually started employing family members, friends and others who came from India and Pakistan. They offered them flexible working shifts to facilitate prayers and time off if there were important family requirements such as medical appointments. The most popular work was in bed manufacturing and furniture factories and many Asians opened large furniture showrooms. Restaurants and takeaways were also fast-growing businesses, so the Asian community built up networks to be independent and become self-sufficient.

There were growing demands for plumbers, joiners, electricians, central heating installers, painters, decorators, and builders, so many Asians and some white people were employed by Asian businesses such as in bed manufacturing and the renovation of properties. Asians also worked in takeaways, and restaurants benefited others by living in close-knit communities and not only helped to fulfil their religious and cultural needs but also secured their future in employment, particularly those who had settled in the UK within the last 20 years. The housewives and other women also benefited because they had the same cultural backgrounds and so they bought household goods in bulk, shared them and saved a lot of money.

Whilst the vast majority of the second-generation Asians were more inclined towards education or learning skills and remained in employment and looked after their parents, unfortunately for others despite their efforts to sustain culture and religion and good behaviour the parents were also faced with a new problem which they never expected. That one day their youths would be indulging in taking and selling drugs and being in a gang, driving recklessly, endangering their own lives as well as those of pedestrians and these kinds of behaviour became a real headache for the parents and community. Many youths were lost without the right guidance and careers and were influenced by a negative culture from outside the community. There were the parents

Wealth and Social Divides

who worked hard and was successful in improving the quality of life and there were others who remained unemployed, but in both cases, they had lost the authority over their children. Although in the minority, the young men became victims and the percentage of young men going to prison had increased. There were also some cases of mental illness within the Asian community which was something that was not known in the 60s to 80s because the community had the same thing in common: a simple working-class life with guaranteed jobs in textile factories.

However, for the majority of Asians, there were positive vibes living in harmony and many of the elderly who came to the UK in the 60s either retired or had passed away and the majority of their children were taking care of their parents by either settling close by or living with them, so they didn't have to go into care homes, as the youngsters still respected the parents and took advice from them about family matters. As the Asian youngsters gradually started changing with their youth culture and there was an increase in divorce rates unlike in the past, when a couple got married, they were living a comfortable family and community life and remained married and had children and grandchildren. The forced marriages were being phased out because the youngsters no longer entertained such ideas and were finding partners for themselves at educational institutions, at work or through friends and meeting them at social events and weddings. However, amongst the more traditional conservative parents, although in the minority, they still practised the culture of forced marriages which is a tragedy for every victim, and by its very nature means that many cases go unreported due to the fear of being punished by the family.

This was the beginning of the new identity of 'British' Muslims. For most youngsters, the UK was their home and they never thought of going back to the Indian subcontinent. So, the relationship between people back home and here slowly started to become distant. Those from the UK who invested money back home in land and houses were still going for holidays during the British winter, but they never stayed, apart from a tiny minority of mostly Pakistani elders who wanted to spend their final days there. Many Pakistanis who died in the UK had their bodies flown to Pakistan to be buried. It was in a way a showcase of loyalty to the country, as well as for the benefit of relatives who had remained in Pakistan and who, by this move, could see the face of the deceased and offer prayers. The Indians, on the other hand preferred to bury their loved ones here. Other Asian elders, after spending their entire life in the UK with children and grandchildren and having a wonderful financially secure life, finally decided to accept Britain as their permanent home.

The third generation of Asian youth who grew up here created their own youth culture, such as a fusion of east and west music, known as Bhangra, which some Muslim youngsters listened to, particularly when groups of boys went out driving in fast cars, going for burgers and chips and cokes, pizzas and doner kebabs with energy drinks and they called it 'chilling', but these were in the minority. The majority were working or being financed by well-to-do parents to start their businesses. One particular young man, who had only had a limited education in a small village in India, and was not even able to communicate in English, was working in a textile factory and at the weekend he would sell wallpaper, tiles and paints from home. Later, as demand increased, he rented a small corner shop and continued selling the same goods at the weekend and in the evening.

From the Splendid Sun to the Glorious Pound

Within a year he had bought a small warehouse and continued selling decorating and tiling goods full time. After a couple of years, he expanded the business further by buying a small warehouse in a nearby town and as the business grew, he managed to expand his business in other towns and cities around Yorkshire over ten years. His annual business turnover started multiplying and within fifteen years he had further warehouses around Yorkshire and beyond, dealing in millions of pounds and employing hundreds of workers as labourers.

The majority of these had been in the UK less than ten years, mostly married to British Asian girls, but because they had not had a higher education back home and were not good with the English language these kinds of jobs suited them best, as they were almost guaranteed full-time employment. The owner of the business also gave a lot of money to charities and financed the building of mosques and madrasas, not only in Dewsbury and Batley, but also in other areas such as Leicester and Lancashire where they sponsored the local professional rugby club where players were all whites. He also opened schools in their village in India, providing free education and meals to children from poor families, paying for their education and helping the poor by building houses.

Here in the UK so far, the Asians particularly the Muslims were more family and community-oriented due to a very closed community set-up. Therefore, children had more respect for their elders and took care of ageing parents in their own homes until they died, and the children also benefited hugely with the moral and financial support from elders. However, in contrast, the changing youth cultures for the third generation and with the demands of modern days living was having an impact on traditional families, as the youths focused on individualism and so, with the pressure of the growing demands of modern living they did not have much time for the extended families and ageing parents. By now there were a few Asian millionaires in Dewsbury and Batley, and the numbers of luxuries, houses and cars increased. However, although there were people with different status and class, one thing they all had in common was that they were not suffering the hardships that their parents and grandparents had suffered back in the Indian subcontinent as well as when they first arrived as immigrants to the UK.

From the Splendid Sun to the Glorious Pound

Here, they were all blessed with a free health service, guaranteed incomes, good quality of food and they were able to afford holidays, not just in the Indian subcontinent, but middle East and being Muslims, they culturally and religiously were able to identify with the people in these countries. Back in India and Pakistan, their grandparents were not able to go on pilgrimage to Makkah in Saudi Arabia, and those poverty-stricken families who did, had to save for a lifetime as they were not supposed to borrow any money and had to pay any debts before going to fulfil one of the commands of Islam, going on Hajj (pilgrimage) following in the footsteps of the Prophet Muhammad at least once in a lifetime. Whereas in the UK, both young and old were able to go on the Hajj pilgrimage more than once and go on Umrah regularly (the word 'Umrah' in Arabic means 'visiting spiritual places'). The name was given to a pilgrimage to Makkah, a shorter version of the annual Hajj gathering. Umrah offers an opportunity for Muslims to refresh their faith, seek forgiveness and pray for their needs.

This they saw as a blessing from God which rewarded them with spiritual life. All this happened because successive British governments invited them to the country and gave

Wealth and Social Divides

them employment and British citizenship, for which they have repaid the British people by working and helping the British economy. They have continued working long and unsociable hours often seven days a week, particularly in the catering business. The first generations of Asians who came after the 60s have retired and a few have passed away. Former members of the Asian Youth Organisation who were community and social workers, have got together and formed an Asian Day Centre, where the elderly seniors including Bashir are invited to participate in social activities and have food. Health workers come to talk about a healthy lifestyle, they participate in physical exercise and are taken out to places of interests around the UK, which they did not have the time to explore earlier as they were working such long hours. It is also a nostalgic time for them, to talk about India and Pakistan and being in the UK as well as the time they have spent working and their achievements. After so many years they've still have not lost their sense of humour and their brotherly friendships continue. Many of the elderly enjoy their retirement within their close-knit Asian community and are taken care of by their children, either staying with them or in the same neighbourhoods. During

From the Splendid Sun to the Glorious Pound

holidays, they would return home, empowered by their savings, pensions and support from their children. This newfound financial stability enabled them to savour meals, explore new destinations, and live in the homes they had constructed. They were therefore able to reclaim the experiences they had missed during their earlier years of scarcity while residing in India or Pakistan. Moreover, they have maintained their traditions of embarking on a pilgrimage to Makkah in Saudi Arabia or visiting the holy place of the Al Aqsa Mosque in Jerusalem.

As time went by, a growing number of the second and third generation of Dewsbury and Batley Muslims were becoming more religious and started changing how they dressed. This was not confined just to this area but also occurred in other towns and cities with close-knit Muslim communities. The men wore Islamic clothes such as kufi caps (a brimless, short, and rounded cap) and a thobe (a long robe) - the top is usually tailored like a shirt, but it is ankle-length and loose. Muslim women would wear the hijab, niqab or burqa and there are lots of other different kinds of coverings worn by Muslim women all over the world. The hijab is a headscarf that covers the hair, neck, and sometimes a woman's shoulders and chest. The burqa is an enveloping garment that comes in a variety of designs, but typically covers a woman's face and head entirely and may cover most or all the rest of her body. Some Muslim women wear full-body garments that only expose their eyes. This is not obligatory in front of her father, brothers, grandfathers, uncles, or young children. Both young men and women started wearing fashionable contemporary Islamic clothes of different colours but maintained the Islamic guidance for a dress code, whereas the elderly normally wore traditional simple black or white colours.

There were increases in the percentage of women wearing veils and hijabs, although critics of the Muslim veiling tradition argue that women do not wear the veil by choice but are often forced to cover their heads and bodies. In contrast, many daughters of Muslim immigrants in the west argued that the veil symbolises devotion and piety and, as they had also started adopting a more spiritual lifestyle, that veiling is their own choice and that to them, it is a question of religious identity and self-expression. At the same time, with the growing population and the pressure of modern living, there were problems of the divorce rate increasing and, although this is not as high as the national average, it is still devastating news for a community based on a nuclear and extended family, and harmonious life without divorce for the past thirty years, which is typical when people migrate to a land with a different culture and changing society.

Also, in the past, the social services and the police hardly had to get involved with family issues at all, as the Asian community looked after their own affairs, but between the 80s and 90s there were some cases of domestic violence and divorces where the social workers were supporting the victims and, if it was necessary, rehoused the families. In many cases, the community elders and leaders helped to sort out problems of family conflicts, just like they traditionally did back home if it was not a legal family matter. Such changes in the Asian community led to some second-generation Asians getting interested in pursuing careers in social, community and youth services This was a great help to the local authorities as well the Asian families because the Asian professionals helped to bridge the gap of understanding Asian culture and language problems.

However, there were a few members of the Asian

Wealth and Social Divides

community who frowned upon the authority getting involved in family matters and saw it as interfering with their culture and religion. This was due to a lack of understanding of the changing Asian culture. The victims were mainly women, and, in some cases, they had to be taken to a refuge with their children to protect them against their husbands who might seek revenge on those who got divorced. Very small numbers got remarried and the majority stayed as single parents and concentrated on bringing up children and educating them well to secure their future. With lessons learnt from their experience of being the victims of domestic violence, they made sure that their children got married according to their own choice. They were so grateful to the British system for supporting and protecting the victims of domestic abuse so they could live life in comfort where their children respected and looked after them. With support from the community and extended family members, the children were brought up to be respectful without being psychologically disturbed unlike in some cases where there was no such support, and the family may have been socially isolated.

The racism continued and the extreme right-wing

organisations once again rose to some extent and tried to become mainstream politicians, without much success however, because the white community have learned to live with Asians and got to know them better after enjoying services such as taxis, restaurants, and takeaways. There were exceedingly small numbers of white people who were still against the Asians being in the UK, and those were motivated by jealousy rather than hate, which was the case in the past when they used to attack Asians physically. In fact, this did not worry Asians who were moving forward in the land which they had accepted as their home, with no intention of returning to India and Pakistan permanently. They wanted to stay here for their children and grandchildren and the financial security of having savings and a state pension.

The perceptions many Asians had at first of having an insecure future in the UK due to different colours, religions, cultures, and racism was fast decreasing, and the feeling of belonging back home started declining too, although they would visit back home for emotional reasons because they or their parents were born there. It was high time for them to move on and, by now, they felt more British and at home here than ever before. Their appreciation and gratitude towards the indigenous population and the British government allowing Asians to treat Britain as their homeland. The Asians were being appreciated on the other hand by the indigenous community and government for their contribution towards the British way of life. So, it was a reassuring lifestyle, and they did not have to worry about being deported like in Africa and Burma and it would be right to assume that thoughts of not belonging here were a thing of the past. Also, in the last few years, they were witnessing technologies that had a profound impact on society: computers have revolutionised lives beyond imagination and continue to play an important role in lives and behaviour. So, this technological revolution benefited them just as the British industrial revolutions in the 1960s benefited their parents and grandparents.

Overall, it was a learning process for all the parties, the Asians became the victims of racism at work, in the streets, and institutionally in the past but now it has significantly reduced. The politicians did not have any clear ideas on how to tackle the issues facing the Asians, and the indigenous population just saw the migrants as taking their jobs and felt they were being swamped by people of different cultures, until they came to realise how much the Asians contributed towards the British economy. Hence, the Labour government led by Prime Minister Tony Blair opened the door and invited in more migrants from the Indian Subcontinent in the 1990s. In 1997, net immigration had been 48,000, but it rose extremely rapidly over the next 12 months, almost trebling, to 140,000 in 1998. It was never to fall below 100,000 again.

Whilst they were enjoying these happy times, unfortunately, like in the past, something came to haunt them once again. One day in September 2001 what is known as 9/11, radical Muslim terrorists attacked the world Trade Centre towers in America. This sent shock waves throughout the world. The Muslims in Britain would once again start asking themselves questions about their future here and the stability of their future. Would there be reprisals? How would their children be treated at school? Could they even be deported? These kinds of thoughts were to be expected due to the Asians' experience of racism in the UK. However, one thing they always relied upon was the thought that they had persevered through so many shocks and tribulations over the last 40 years. As the time passed, they continued with their lifestyle as they had done in the past, but with caution. Questions remained in their minds despite their struggle to earn a secure future in the UK, what would happen to the future generations? However, despite all this, looking at what the immigrants had achieved so far by being in the UK and how it had helped to reshape their lives with better prospects, once again their faith in the British people and the government remained the focal point of their confidence.

The 2001 UK census showed 3.9% of the population to be 'Asian' or 'British Asian' (just over 2.3 million people). This included first, second and third-generation settlers. Although some have retained strong links with families and places in South Asia, they think of themselves as British Pakistanis, British Bangladeshis, or British Indians. Most of them have already adopted Britain as their homeland. After all, such were the dreams and ambitions of their parents and grandparents and this success is reflected in their new-found confidence. Like others, the newer generations acknowledged historical heritage or religion as part of their identity, but, nevertheless, would treat Britain as their birthplace with both its weaknesses and strengths. However, the strengths of most Asians were that, just like the indigenous community, they would take an interest in every sphere of the British way of life whether that was economically, politically, or socially. The second and particularly the third generation Asians have learnt to interact with the native British and share similar interests and this made it easier for them to socialise. They will co-exist alongside other communities, which will help to improve race and community relations with the vast majority naturally helping to raise the profile of Britain nationally and internationally, so much so that when they go abroad, they take pride in showing their British passports to relatives and neighbours.

Chapter Thirteen

Journey's End

In reviewing the experiences, accomplishments, and relationships that make up the life of the Asian migrant in the UK, it is apparent that their distinct features, reasoning, spirit, and religious faith kept them together as a community and most importantly Britain gives them the right to practice their religion as they please. They coexist alongside the white community, removing the fear of losing their cultural identity and economic achievement, which reaffirm their desire to remain in the UK.

Despite successfully achieving a better way of life in the UK, the life they once lived in India and Pakistan slowly diminished as the years passed by. Up to the 1980s and early 1990s, a family member living in the UK used to be seen as a person with superior status by the people back at home who were relying on relatives from the UK for financial support. When the British Asians went back to India as visitors the relatives and friends from the village would go to receive them at the railway station with garlands made of flowers. The people from the village would visit them and queue up

From the Splendid Sun to the Glorious Pound

to invite them for dinner. The British Asians would be dressed in western fashionable clothes and take gifts such as clothes, chocolates and many other British memorabilia for the friends and members of family who were really impressed by such generosity. The Pakistanis in the UK on the other hand were allowed to hold dual nationalities by Pakistan and the elders were still well connected and would regularly visit Pakistan. Whereas the Indians were treated by the Indian authorities as Non-Resident Indians (NRI), which meant they could not stay there indefinitely, had no voting rights, and had to apply for visas unless they applied for an OCI (Overseas Citizenship of India) Card a multi-purpose, multiple entry, life-long visa. Furthermore, the new generation of British Indians with different customs, habits, language barriers and the growing numbers of youths who were reluctant to marry girls from India, gradually started distancing themselves. Whereas some of the new generations of Pakistanis were still influenced by parents and would marry in Pakistan.

The Asian migrants have come a long way from the time when they had to face hardship, discrimination, social isolation, and poverty and are now proud to regard Britain as

Journey's End

their permanent home. The second and third generations have enjoyed both Western and Asian cultures and shared common interests such as arts, careers, sports, and politics. They do not often have to think about their identity like their parents, although it does not change the fact that they still feel comfortable identifying themselves with their own religious and cultural identity. Finally, the Asians have become part of the UK. Bashir retired and, along with Amina, spent more time with family, particularly with their grandchildren. Like so many other parents, Bashir and Amina have helped their children financially and made their life much easier in comparison with life when they were young and when the children started earning, they supported their parents like many second-generation Asians. Later, as time passed, Bashir and many of his companions regularly spent time at the Asian Day Centre and continued visiting places of interest in the UK. Amina and her companions too, although separately, were going to places like Bashir was. In fact, they would say to their children jokingly that they had visited more places throughout the UK than the men had. Whilst most Asians were victims of poverty, those who were running businesses saw their children expand the businesses even further. Riaz, Bashir's cousin, had expanded and established wholesale businesses in America and like them, many youngsters who were educated and became professionals were also enjoying a prosperous lifestyle.

The Asians were finally recognised by the trades unions as being part of the British class system, which includes the upper class, normally people with inherited wealth, the middle class along with most of the population of the UK, and the lower or working class, which includes blue-collar workers, both white and Asian. However, being in another country as a migrant always poses the question of what their fate will be in the future in the UK. They take solace from their experiences of the struggles and challenges they have faced in trying to make Britain their home and that dream has become reality. The Muslim community continued building mosques and offering people the chance to come together with the opportunity to reflect on themselves and focus on their spiritual goals. For them, it is important to remove any misconceptions around Islam, change any negative perspectives that people may have of it and to remain respectable citizens of Britain. Additionally, the resilience of the English people and successive governments

Journey's End

have allowed laws to be passed that protect Muslims against discrimination and given them the reassurance to continue living in Britain with dignity.

Printed in Great Britain
by Amazon